THE
MISSING
WIDOW

BOOKS BY L.G. DAVIS

Liar Liar

Perfect Parents

My Husband's Secret

The Stolen Breath

Don't Blink

The Midnight Wife

The Janitor's Wife

THE MISSING WIDOW

L.G. DAVIS

bookouture

Published by Bookouture in 2022

An imprint of Storyfire Ltd.
Carmelite House
50 Victoria Embankment
London EC4Y 0DZ

www.bookouture.com

ISBN: 978-1-80314-675-1
eBook ISBN: 978-1-80314-674-4

This book is a work of fiction. Names, characters, businesses, organizations, places and events other than those clearly in the public domain, are either the product of the author's imagination or are used fictitiously. Any resemblance to actual persons, living or dead, events or locales is entirely coincidental.

For Toye. I love you more.

CHAPTER 1

In less than a year, my husband Brett will be gone. He will leave me, and the world, forever. So every moment I have with him now is precious, and I want this time to stretch out into eternity. I grasp hold of every sensation, absorbing all the details. His hand is warm against my palm. His fingers are slender, strong, still full of life. My bare feet press into the soft gray and white carpet underneath the glass dining table, and I turn to look outside as I try to hold back the tears. The sky above Fort Haven, our little town in North Carolina, is awash in purple, orange, and pink hues as dusk settles.

We're in the dining room, with its large French windows open, overlooking our backyard so that a cool breeze drifts toward us. It has always been my favorite room. The garden reminds me of the fairy-tale magic I imagined in nature as a child, especially in summer when I sit out with a drink in hand. The yard is filled with sweet-smelling shrubs and flowers, many of which I have planted myself. Normally, I love to look out at the trees, which are clustered together at the back of our property, especially the hickory whose giant branches span out wide, reaching up into the sunlight. Often there's a squirrel or two, jumping from branch to branch or scampering across the ground.

This room is the perfect place to take a moment and appreciate the beauty of life, to imprint a memory I will cherish forever. But my mind won't allow me that mercy, and this evening, even our lovely garden fills me with sorrow. The trees cast dark shadows across the grass, the birds' evening song seems strained and wavering, and the clusters of bright summer flowers remind me of wreaths. Even gazing out, on what I know must be a beautiful summer's evening, I feel like everything is in mourning already, tainted by the impending death of my husband.

On the table, the wine I poured for us sits untouched. A drink would soothe my dry throat, but I'm too anxious to take one, with my stomach tightly knotted. I turn back to Brett and watch his face, which is bathed in warm light from the overhead pendant lamp. Trying to comfort me, he smiles and squeezes my hand, and I smile because I'm trying to comfort him right back, even though I know I'm probably failing too. I can't bear the thought of losing him, of having our family torn apart.

To make matters worse, when he dies, I will have no one to turn to for comfort. No close friends, and no family. My parents died in a car accident when I was eighteen. It was a cold Wednesday morning, two weeks before Christmas, and I was leaving the Fundamentals of Accounting lecture at the University of North Carolina in Charlotte when I got the call that tore my world apart. Unable to win against the depression that plagued me following my parents' deaths, I dropped out of college and moved back to Fort Haven to be with my grandmother, leaving behind my new university life and my friends, who soon forgot about me.

After years of pain and loneliness, Brett was my new beginning, my fairy tale. But fairy tales don't exist, not in my world. I was a fool to believe they did.

Right now, I'm trying hard to be strong for both of us, but I'm slowly coming undone.

"Are you okay, Meghan?" Brett lifts a thick eyebrow. His voice is deep with exhaustion.

Since his stomach cancer diagnosis one month ago, Brett tires more easily. I'm afraid that doesn't stop him from giving the little energy he has left to the Fort Haven-based Black Oyster Resort, one in a chain of his family's luxury hotels, and where we met. His father had hired me to work as a maid, and Brett and I fell in love and got married within six months.

Brett works incredibly hard, and it often feels like business comes first, even before our little family. Whenever I confront him about this, he denies it, but it's the truth. I thought I was okay with getting the scraps of his time, and I forced myself to be grateful for having him in my life at all. But not anymore, not when we have such little time left together. Today is our wedding anniversary and I so badly want us to create one last happy memory. For just a few hours, I want to live in denial, to pretend our life is perfect even though it's far from it.

But before I can answer his question, Brett's phone beeps. He always answers his calls, especially when it's his mother. Every time she calls, he jumps.

I tighten my fingers around his. "Don't," I whisper, knowing full well that I'm asking for the impossible. "Don't answer it, please."

His gaze moves to the phone nestled between his glass of white wine and his plate of uneaten hake.

"Sorry, sweetheart. It's my mom; you know I have to answer." He wipes his mouth and tosses his napkin onto the table, then reaches for the phone to speak to my mother-in-law.

Nora Wilton is a quintessential control freak. She struggles to accept that her only son is a grown man, and that he married a woman from a lower class. Her husband, Cole, is not as intrusive as she is, but he can still be quite difficult and demanding, and I hate how Brett is always anxious and helpless around them.

Brett once told me that, as a child, his dream was to become a doctor, but he didn't because his parents pushed him to join the family business. I always wonder if he feels regretful when he plays doctor games with Ashton. He may not have become a doctor, but sometimes it's as if he lives the life of one. He gets a call and a few minutes later he's gone. It doesn't matter what time of day or night it is.

My in-laws have never welcomed me with open arms, and Nora loves to show up unannounced from time to time, reminding me that the luxury two-story house we live in belongs to them, that I'm just a guest. Five months ago, without my permission or even discussing it with me, she had decorators come to our home to renovate our master bedroom, including replacing all the old furniture, some of which I had picked out personally from thrift shops and antique stores. I felt as power-less as I was astounded. She went all out with luxurious fabrics in royal blue and beige, white furniture and bedding, and new crystal chandeliers above our bed and in the lounge area.

I've tried hard to blend in with the décor, but it feels as if I'm wearing a ridiculously expensive and uncomfortable dress. Nothing is to my taste; it all just reminds me of her. When I confronted her about redecorating without consulting us first, she said I should stop being ungrateful and learn to appreciate her generosity, that she was doing it for her son.

She never wanted me to marry Brett and she made that abundantly clear the morning of our wedding day, when she pulled me aside and threatened to destroy our marriage if I didn't walk away. Of course, I went ahead and married Brett anyway, but nothing was ever the same. Our marriage was poisoned before it even started.

After the wedding, I was desperate to get away, and I begged Brett to walk away from Fort Haven so we could start a new life in another town. I even proposed that we move to another Black Oyster Hotel location, so he could continue to work in the family business, but Brett dismissed the idea immediately. His parents needed him in Fort Haven, he said.

The truth is that Nora has always wanted to have him close enough to control, and Brett was never going to stand up to her. There have been many times I resented him for it, but my love for him made me stay. He needed me. He *needs* me.

While Brett is on the phone, I sigh heavily, fold up my own napkin and push myself to my feet. Trying to push my frustration down, I head upstairs to check on Ashton, our four-year-old son.

I meet Jane, our live-in housekeeper, at the top of the sweeping stairs. At thirty-five, Jane is three years older than me, but she already has noticeable wrinkles at the corners of her dark-brown eyes and around her thin lips. She's a stunning woman with big eyes and lashes that don't need mascara to make them stand out. The dark goddess braid she always wears to work, and the elegant way she moves, make her look royal in my eyes.

"Ashton is already asleep," she whispers, her face blank. Watching her cool eyes meet mine, I ignore the ache of rejection in my heart.

Jane and I first met when we worked together at the hotel. Something about her just connected with me and we became very close, but our friendship ended as soon as I married Brett and he hired her to be our housekeeper. I didn't need the help, but his parents insisted that we should find someone. Since then, Jane has been polite and respectful toward me but also a little distant, sometimes with palpable tension. I miss my friend, and every time she addresses me as "Mrs. Wilton" it jars.

I asked Brett if we could have another housekeeper instead of my friend, but he told me that the hotel was making cuts and this would be a way to keep her in employment. Jane is great at her job, too, and always goes above and beyond, sometimes even taking on the role of a nanny to our son. I tell her often that looking after Ashton is not part of her job, but she insists that she likes to keep busy. And since Ashton clearly loves spending time with her, I let her do it.

Once or twice a week, Jane also works a couple of hours at the hotel. I wish I had the power to increase her income, so she wouldn't need to work in two locations, but it's Brett's parents who pay her. I'm glad she at least agreed to stay with us, so she doesn't need to worry about her living expenses.

"Thank you, Jane. It's best I don't disturb him, then. There's really nothing more for you to do tonight. We're not going out anymore, so you don't have to babysit. You can call it a day if you like. Go and get some rest."

After the anniversary dinner I cooked for us, Brett had planned on taking me to a concert, but I already know that this will be one of the many, many dates that will be canceled because of his parents' interference. Nora knows full well that today is our anniversary and I'm certain she called to mess with our plans.

Jane nods and for a moment she gazes at my face, as if she is studying it. "Goodnight, Mrs. Wilton," she says finally, and my heart sinks. I was starting to become hopeful that she might say something more personal, something that would show a willingness to rekindle our friendship.

I force a smile. "Goodnight, Jane. Thanks for everything."

Instead of returning downstairs, I head over to our bedroom and sit on the edge of the king-size bed, my hands pressed into the snow-white comforter, my eyes burning with unshed tears.

I try not to think about how our lives will be when Brett is no longer here. He lives each day pretending the cancer is not real, and every time I mention it, he checks out of the conversation. He hasn't even told his parents and he made me promise not to either. I wish he would fight for his life, but he refuses to undergo chemotherapy, even though the doctors say he might be able to add a few more months or even years to his thirty-six. Brett's reasoning is that there's no guarantee that it will work, and that he heard about the impact of chemotherapy and doesn't want that for himself. I can understand why he wouldn't want his final months to be so drawn out and uncomfortable, but I just wish we had more time.

I look up, hearing a soft knock on the door. Brett is standing in the doorway, his phone in his hand. "I'm so sorry, baby," he says. "I have to go to the hotel. We need to postpone our date, there's an emergency."

I already expected him to cancel, so I merely nod and try to pretend I'm not disappointed. The last thing I want to do with him now is to fight.

"What kind of emergency?" I ask, deflated. "I thought it was your mother who called."

"Yes, and then Dad got on the phone and told me about some employee issues we're having. Nothing that can't be sorted out."

"I see. Did someone else quit?"

In the past month two housekeepers have resigned, and I can't help but wonder if Nora is to blame. Cole and Nora live in a mansion only a block away from the hotel, and while Nora is dedicated to her philanthropic work, she's also constantly at the hotel looking over the employees' shoulders, making sure things are done to her high standards and screaming at them when they're not.

"Yeah." Brett rubs the back of his neck. He looks so tired, and I want to draw him into my arms, but as I look at him and try to keep my emotions in check, I can't pretend to myself that I'm not frustrated. Today is probably the last anniversary we will have together.

"Can't your father handle it himself?" I don't understand why Cole always feels the need to call Brett.

"No. It's important that I'm there." Brett shoves his phone into his pocket. "I won't be long, I promise." He crosses the room and comes to kiss the tip of my nose.

"Don't be long," I call after him. "I'll wait up for you."

The door closes behind him and, a few minutes later, his Cadillac Escalade roars to life.

I remain sitting on my bed listening to the silence, my eyes closed, tears slipping through my eyelids. Then I fall back onto the bed and fall asleep in my canary-yellow cocktail dress, the one I chose because I know Brett loves it.

It feels like no time has passed at all when Brett wakes me up as he comes back in, his curly dark hair as rumpled as his shirt. But the first thing I do is glance at the clock. It's five minutes to midnight. He left at eight.

"Hey." I try to swallow down my annoyance and hurt at our lost evening. Brett looks so tired and pale. He probably had a fight with his father. Or he might be in pain.

He doesn't respond at all as he walks over to his side of the bed and removes his socks.

"Was it something serious?" I ask, going to massage his shoulders. I'm surprised when he flinches a little.

He gets to his feet and my hands drop from his shoulders. "Yeah," he says and disappears

through the sliding doors of the walk-in closet, which always feels outrageously luxurious to me with its thick, white, shaggy carpeting, mirrored walls, gold accents, and cream leather chairs. He slides the frosted-glass doors closed and remains in there for almost fifteen minutes. Figuring that he needs to be alone, I change into my nightgown and wait for him under the covers in case he wants to talk later.

When he comes out of the closet, he's wearing his pajamas and the expression on his face is even more broken than before.

For a few heartbeats, he stands in the middle of the room and stares at me.

"What's wrong, Brett? You're scaring me. Did you have an argument with your father?"

He nods and finally climbs into bed, and I don't push him for more answers. I hate Cole even more than Nora right now for ruining our anniversary, for taking him away from me yet again. I rest my head on my husband's chest, listening to his heartbeat and wondering how many of them are still left.

"I need you to promise me one thing," he says suddenly.

"Okay," I whisper and hold my breath.

"Don't let the cancer eat me alive," he says in a choked voice.

"What... what are you saying?" I sit up and search his eyes.

"When it gets to be too much, when I'm too weak, I want you..." Words fail him as he bites his lip, still staring ahead. "Help me die with dignity."

For what feels like an hour, I can't move or breathe.

"Did you hear me?" he asks, finally looking at me.

"No." I shake my head, tears spilling from my eyes. "I don't understand."

"You do." He turns to face me and gazes deep into my eyes. "When I reach the end, I want you to help me die. Please."

"You want me to kill you?" I'm shocked that those words are even leaving my lips.

"I want you to help me," he says, his voice suddenly cracking as it raises slightly. "If you really love me, you will do it."

CHAPTER 2

Two months have passed since Brett asked me to do the unthinkable, and I'm still reeling with shock. The day after, he told me exactly how he wanted to go. He said he wanted to die on his own terms; he didn't want cancer to win. I listened without interrupting him, praying that he would change his mind.

I'm afraid to raise it with him, and I don't know if he has changed his mind. He has been deteriorating so swiftly in the last few weeks, and sometimes he's so silent and withdrawn that it feels like he's already gone. He has even distanced himself from Ashton, and sometimes I think he's pulling away to prepare us for a life without him. Almost every day I beg him to accept treatment that might extend his life, but it just makes him angry.

He begged me not to tell his parents about his illness; he said that he would do so when he was ready, but Nora found out two days ago. I think she forced it out of Brett, when she saw how his weight was melting off and his eyes and cheeks were sinking into his skull.

Not long ago, Jane answered the door and Nora burst into

the dining room just as we were finishing up with dinner, demanding to speak to him. She looked no-nonsense in a black suit with a white button-up shirt and her dark hair cut bluntly at her shoulders. She never wears any jewelry, except for a large diamond ring on her left hand. The first time I met Nora, the first thing that came to my mind was that she looks and sounds like a school principal.

"I want to be alone with my son," she said, her cool blue-green eyes fixed on me.

"Of course, Nora." I left the room to give them some time alone, but now I'm standing with my ear to the wooden door as I strain to hear their conversation. It's getting more and more heated by the second. As much as I dislike Nora, I'm hoping that maybe Brett will listen to her.

"You will fight this thing," Nora is ordering him. "You need to be a man and do whatever it takes to survive. Take the treatment. You're a father, so don't act like a selfish little boy."

I press my back against the wall next to the kitchen door and squeeze my eyes shut. The force of Nora's harsh words bruises even me, but, right now, I just want Brett to live and I'm praying Nora will get through to him.

"Mom, you have no right to tell me what to do about my health. I know you like to have your way, but not this time. This is my life and my decision." Brett's words are edged with steel. "Now if you don't mind, I'd like to be alone."

My heart jumps to my throat when I hear something smash, the scream of glass shattering against a hard surface, perhaps the glass Brett was drinking water from a little while ago.

"How dare you speak to me with such disrespect?" Nora grinds the words out between her teeth. "You stupid boy. After everything I've done for you, the least you can do is listen to me."

A part of me is proud that Brett is finally standing up to his mother. But I wish it wasn't over this.

Brett laughs. "You think you control me, don't you? Well, you don't. This is my choice, not yours and not Dad's."

"The hell it is," Nora snaps. "You will have chemo and that's the end of it."

Then the door flies open and she storms out. It's too late for me to make an escape.

Her eyes are spitting fire when they meet mine, and a vein is pulsing in her neck. "We need to talk," she orders, and I step away from her. "Let's go to the office."

My chest filling with anxiety, I do as I'm told and, when she opens the door, I'm surprised to find Cole waiting inside, looking out of the window. He turns and moves toward us, leaning a hand on the heavy oak desk. Cole has a slight limp when he walks, and Brett told me it was from an accident he had as a child. In his early sixties, Cole is a tall but nondescript kind of man, not someone you'd easily pick out from a crowd. But despite his average looks, he usually carries himself in a confident and commanding way, drawing the attention of anyone around him. Today, though, he just looks tired, with his light-brown hair in disarray, his face strained, and his navy-blue tie wrinkled and loose around his neck.

He nods briefly in my direction, then his slate-gray gaze goes to his wife. "Did you talk sense into him, or should I try?"

Ignoring him, Nora slams the door shut and turns on me. "Brett is still refusing to have any treatment, and it's your fault."

"Come on now, Nora," Cole says, leading his wife toward a black leather couch. "Throwing accusations isn't going to do Brett any good. Let's all sit down and figure out how we can get him to see reason."

Cole sits next to Nora and asks me to sit as well, but I shake my head and jam my hands into my armpits. "No, I prefer to stand. Nora, what exactly are you accusing me of?"

"I'm accusing you of doing nothing to save my son," she says, her nostrils flaring. "I need to know why you kept Brett's cancer from us. You should have told me as soon as he was diagnosed. And you should have persuaded him to seek treatment. You're his wife; if my son dies, it will be on you." She narrows her eyes. "Or is that what you want?"

I feel the blood drain from my face. "How could you say something like that? I love Brett with all my heart. I want him to live as much as you do. It hurts me that—"

"Can't you see how selfish you are being?" she interrupts, tears spilling from her eyes. "You should have told me what was wrong with my son."

"Now, now, let's all just calm down." Cole puts a hand on Nora's shoulder, but she shrugs him off.

"No, Cole, I won't calm down." She glares at him. "How can you be so blind? Don't you see what she's trying to do? She doesn't love our son, and she never has. She wants him to die so she can inherit his fortune. Isn't that right, Meghan?" Nora's tone is as sharp as knives. "If you love him as you claim that you do, you would have forced him to seek treatment. But you didn't. You just sat back and watched him waste away."

My chest seizes and I gasp from shock and pain. Her accusations are so vicious that the air around me evaporates. "That's not true at all," I whisper. I want to say more, but I'm finding it hard to defend myself when my voice is so weak. "You're wrong about me, Nora. I do love Brett and I would never ever want to see him dead." I shake my head. "It's Brett who doesn't want to get treatment, not me. I wish he would..." My voice trails off and I drop my head, staring at the floor, trying not to fall to pieces.

Cole starts to speak, but Nora cuts him off. "Don't be fooled by her crocodile tears, Cole. She's trying to play us like fools. If I didn't coax the truth out of Brett, that woman would have let him die. We would not have even known until it's too late."

I drop my hands to my sides and curl them into fists of rage. I want to shoot her a scathing remark, but the words freeze inside my throat as they so often do in a conversation with her.

"It's not... you know—" I take a breath and try again. "Nora, Brett asked me not to tell you. He's my husband and I respect his wishes."

"He's my son, damn you. You should have told me. I knew from the start that you were bad news."

Cole fiddles with his Rolex, looking down at the carpet. "Meghan, you need to understand that we're just very worried about our son," he says sadly. "Please do everything you can to convince him to seek treatment. We will pay for everything."

"I can't promise you that, Cole. I've tried countless times and failed."

"We're not asking you, Meghan," Nora cuts in. "This is an order. Talk to him tonight. We'll arrange for one of the best doctors in the country to see him in the next few days. Make sure Brett is resting and eating well, if you're capable of taking care of him at all."

Her face is hard as she pushes to her feet and storms toward the door, followed by Cole. Without another word to me, they walk out, and the front door slams shut. I remain inside the office for a few minutes, drawing in calming breaths before I go to see Brett.

I find him in our bedroom, lying flat on our bed. "Whatever my parents want, I hope you told them they can go to hell." Groaning, he rolls to his side first, then sits up. "Meghan, when will you make it go away?"

CHAPTER 3

I tried, I really did. I used every ounce of persuasion I could muster to try to convince Brett to seek help, but I failed. He won't listen to me or his parents, who are not used to being defied by him. As a result, I get to feel his mother's fury. Nora is still convinced that I'm the reason her son is suffering and that I want him gone. Her vile accusations have left me emotionally, mentally, and physically drained to the point that, sometimes, I can barely function.

A few hours ago, Nora and Cole came over as they do every day and Nora was beside herself when she saw him. She demanded he go into hospital, but Brett adamantly refused, just as he would not see any of the specialists they have sent to the house in recent weeks. In the end, she just broke down.

After a little while, Brett asked to speak to his mother alone. From downstairs, I could hear her crying hysterically at his bedside while Cole paced the living room back and forth, until Brett asked to speak to him on his own too. When they were done, Cole just looked angry, furious at death, at God, at the universe, for taking his son away so soon. I understand. They don't seem to realize I'm in pain too, that I am with them... that we're drowning together in an ocean of grief. I wish they saw me, so that we could support each other in some way.

When they left, I could hear Nora crying all the way to the car. Jane was in the garden with Ashton, and I watched them for a while, tears running silently down my cheeks. I splashed cold water over my face in the bathroom before going outside to join them, attempting to act happy and normal for my son.

Now, after giving Ashton a bath and helping him put on his pajamas, I get into my nightgown and return to the kitchen to find Jane washing up the dishes. I'm desperate to speak to her, to rebuild the broken bridge between us. I miss her deeply, and I could really use a friend like her right now, she was once always so empathetic and warm. I especially need that warmth after today when Brett's condition seemed to have rapidly worsened over the course of only a few hours. No matter how hard I try to reach him, he keeps going deeper and deeper into the darkness. Every time I see him, I feel my heart gradually breaking apart, and it hurts even more each time he asks me to end his pain.

"Jane," I say softly as she turns around and faces me. "Can we talk for a minute?"

She sets down the sponge, stares at me for a moment or two, and nods slowly. "Is there anything else you want me to do before I retire to my room?"

I swallow hard and wrap my arms around my body, feeling as though the breeze making its way through the window has chilled before touching my skin. "No, I... it's nothing to do with chores. I just wanted to talk like we used to... as friends."

"Oh," she says and turns back to the sink. I stand there and watch her go back to washing the dishes, noticing the way her hands shake. Finally, she takes a deep breath and turns to face me. "I'm sorry, Meghan, but we're not friends anymore. You're my boss. You made a choice."

"Jane, please. I never wanted our friendship to end." I walk toward her and stop at the edge of the kitchen table. "Why are you still punishing me for falling in love and—"

"Mrs. Wilton, I'm sorry you're going through a hard time with your husband being sick and all, but I'm here to work, not to socialize."

I blink hard, trying to clear the tears from my eyes. "I understand."

But I don't. I can't see why she's still so bitter about me marrying our boss' son, but when Brett and I got together, she and our friend Denise, who, thanks to me, also found work as a maid at the hotel, saw it as a kind of betrayal. Maybe because I was becoming "one of them": a wealthy and privileged person who was rich off the back of their labor. But I would have thought that they'd see I was falling in love, that Brett's wealth didn't matter to me at all. That I was the same person they'd always known. The three of us used to be so close, close enough for us to share our dreams, our pasts, our secrets.

Jane told me that she used to be a drug addict before she checked herself into a rehab facility in Fort Haven and got sober. Before that, she lived in Willow Creek, Tennessee, a small town a little over three hours' drive away. Her parents wanted her to move away and distance herself from the old friends who had kept her on a path of self-destruction. Since getting clean, she said she never wanted to go back to her home-town and her old ways, not until she was much older. I have always been so impressed by her strength and determination.

The first time I met her, she had come to the hotel looking for a job and I overheard her talking to Brett, who told her there were no open positions. I guess she had been trying her luck everywhere, and when I left work that evening, I found her sitting outside the hotel, smoking a cigarette and crying. She told me she had nowhere to go, and I couldn't just walk away. So, I asked her to stay with me at my place and, the next day, I begged Brett to hire her, just as I had done for Denise about six months earlier. We were not dating at the time, but I knew he had a soft spot for me. He said yes, and a week later Jane and I were colleagues. Very soon, we became fast friends, and room-mates not long after, together with Denise. Then I fell in love, and everything changed.

With my legs tired and heavy, I walk to the door. "I'll go and tuck Ashton in. Have a good night, Jane."

"Goodnight," she says to my back.

Instead of going straight to Ashton's room, I find myself stumbling out of the house and onto the front porch, leaning over the edge of the steps, blinded by my tears.

After a little while, I hear a voice coming from someone walking past the house.

"Meghan, how is Brett? He hasn't taken a turn for the worst, has he?"

I wipe my cheeks and look over at Laurel, who lives next door with her mother, Marjorie. Without being invited, she steps up onto the porch. She must have just come from a late evening jog because she's wearing her running shoes, a tight tank top, and mini shorts. Laurel is tall and slender, with long blonde hair, endless legs, and a round, pretty face. But there's nothing sweet at all about her. Still, she looks fresh and beau-tiful and, in my nightgown and with puffy eyes and dried tears on my cheeks, I feel more than a little self-conscious.

She grew up with Brett and I know from gossip around town that she had always wanted to be more than friends with him, but somehow only found the courage to express those feel-ings after he married me. She has no shame in flirting with him whenever she gets the chance.

Earlier today, after Nora and Cole left, Laurel showed up

with a large bouquet of flowers for Brett. Before I left the room, I saw her hugging him and whispering, loud enough for me to hear, "I'm here for you if you need anything at all, darling... Anything."

I nod and try to calm myself. "Yes, Brett is very ill."

"Oh, God. I want to see him again, please," she says, pressing her French-manicured hand to her chest. "Will you take me to him?"

When she tries to push her way past me, I shake my head. "No, he's really sick, Laurel, and he doesn't want to see anyone right now. He's sleeping. You could come in the morning."

It's not long after seven and I know Brett won't be able to sleep for hours, if the pain lets him at all, but there's no way I'm going to tell her that.

She looks livid, red spots appearing on her cheeks. "You can't keep me away from him, you know. I'll be back to see him, and you can't stop me."

With that she turns around and makes her way down the steps before hurrying off toward her mother's house.

That's when I realize I've been holding my breath. I let it out slowly and head to Ashton's room before going to help Brett through another long night.

I take a moment to compose myself outside his door and enter to find Ashton sitting on his bed, playing with his toy cars.

His grandmother was also responsible for decorating his room, and it feels exaggerated to me, like the set of a children's television show. There's a circus scene on the ceiling, and blue walls with clouds are a backdrop to the single bed in the shape of a car. To be fair, Ashton does love the gigantic train mural, which takes up an entire wall.

"Hey, honey." My voice comes out slightly husky. "Are you ready for bed?"

I sit next to him on the bed and run a hand through his

curly brown hair before kissing his warm cheek, still marked with a faint scar from when he fell from his bike a month ago. It's barely visible now, and most people don't see it, but as his mother, I know it's there.

He tilts his head to the side and his wide gray eyes meet mine.

"I don't want to sleep, Mommy. I'm scared."

My heart clenches and I fight hard to suppress another wave of tears as I gather him up and into my arms, inhaling his scent. If I ask him what he's afraid of, he'll just say he doesn't know. But I know, even if he doesn't. He's picking up on what's happening around him; he knows his father is ill.

"I know you're scared, Superboy, but you are the bravest little boy I know."

"Mommy, is Daddy angry with me?" he whispers.

"Of course not, baby. Don't ever think that." I almost choke on my words as I put both hands on the sides of his soft cherub face. "He loves you so much."

"But he never plays with me anymore." He tucks his lower lip inward and blinks, his lashes long and curly.

"Daddy's very sick, honey," I whisper, and trying to keep my voice from trembling is like trying to hold onto water. "He doesn't have the energy to play right now. But he loves you so much."

I read him a story and tuck him in, then I switch off the light, since Ashton can't sleep with even the slightest bit of light in the room. Before I step out of the room, he grabs hold of my hand.

"Will you stay with me for longer, Mommy?" he asks, his voice trembling. "I'm still scared."

I nod and read him one more story, stroking his hair. By the time I reach the end, he's asleep and I sneak out of the room. I make my way down the hallway, pausing in front of our bedroom door. Then I draw a deep breath and walk in, hoping to find Brett sleeping, finally peaceful. He had been drowsy when I left him. But he's awake now, and immediately I can see that he's really struggling. He's trembling under the covers, his face contorted with pain and covered in a sheen of sweat. I'm used to seeing him in pain by now, and it has never stopped hurting me too, but this time it's different, more intense.

For a moment his eyes widen, and he's gazing in my direction, but he doesn't seem to be seeing me.

"Baby, I'm sorry you're in so much pain." I lie down next to him, putting my arms around his frail body. I think he tries to push me away, but he has barely any strength to move his body, and I bite down hard on my lip to force back the tears.

"I'll get you some meds." I slide off the bed.

"No," he grunts. "No painkillers."

"You need help, baby. I'll take you to the hospital, okay?" I search the room for my handbag, where I left my phone.

"No hospital." This time his tone is hard, final. Then his face crumples with pain again, his eyes squeezed tight. "Help me. *You* help me."

I want to pretend I don't know what he's talking about, but in between the grunts of pain, he spells it out for me.

"I want you to... help... die."

I come back over to the bed. "No, Brett." I cup his sweating face with both hands. My eyes are so blurred that I can barely see his features. "Please don't ask me to do that to you."

"Please." It breaks my heart to see my husband crying like a child, broken by the pain, but I cannot give him the kind of help he wants. The ever-present pain in my chest twists deeper and tears fill my eyes, blurring my vision. Raw agony gnaws at me like a rabid animal.

He continues to beg, and his voice has sunk to a whisper. His gaze is distant again as if he's looking right through me. "I want to die, Meghan." I can hear every murmured word, and I know they will echo in my mind for the rest of my life.

It feels like an eternity passes between us, with my heart swollen and bruised, his moans of pain wounding me forever.

"Okay, Brett," I say finally, and pull away from him as he curls up into a ball. "Okay." Tears are pouring down my face and I don't bother to wipe them away.

Inside my chest, my heart is racing and what feels like molten lava is scorching through my veins. Doing what he wants will end his suffering, but it will kill me inside, scoop out my heart and soul, and leave me a hollow shell. But how could I not want to end the suffering of the man I love?

"Thank you," he chokes as I walk out of the room and head down to the kitchen.

Before I open the medicine cabinet, a sound I can't place catches my attention over my pounding heart. I glance out the window and realize that it must be the branches outside hitting the wall. Some of the trees are getting too big and need pruning.

I shut the blinds and try to steel myself, locking away my emotions. Feeling unsteady on my feet, I grab the counter with my hands, my fingers curling around the marble. Absently, I notice that Jane has forgotten her cell phone; it lies neglected on the counter.

I reach for a dish towel and press it against my eyes, but all I see behind them is Brett's graying face, his pain-filled eyes.

I have to help him.

He told me about a brown paper package in the medicine cabinet, which contains everything I would need to end his life. I never looked inside it until now. I open it to see a page with instructions, and I follow them robotically, my hands moving as if they are not my own.

Once filled, the syringe is light, but it feels heavy in my hand. I don't even know what kind of medication it is, because the packaging is plain white with no name. Brett said an autopsy is unlikely to be carried out, not on a man as close to death as he is.

I pour him a glass of whiskey as he requested, his last drink on Earth, and, in a daze, I take everything upstairs. My feet moving slowly, one in front of the other, I let myself into the room and lock the door behind me. I was only away for a few short minutes, but Brett's body seems even more frail and twisted, his breath strained and ragged.

Seeing him like this is killing me and I try to swallow the lump in my throat, but it's so constricted that I can hardly breathe.

Holding the whiskey in one hand and the syringe in the other, I move toward him and pray for a miracle, a way out.

I offer to help him put the whiskey to his lips as he's too weak even to raise his hand, but he mouths *no*. "Do it now," he croaks. "Plea... please."

But the moment I wrap my hand around his wrist and feel his pulse, I'm catapulted back to my senses.

What am I doing?

"No." I drop his hand again. "No," I repeat.

I can't do it.

I can't bring myself to kill the man I love. I want to make his last days as comfortable as possible, but I can't do this. I can't kill him.

Brett tries to reach for my hand, but he can't. I drop the syringe, shaking, and it falls to the floor next to the nightstand. Slowly, as if I'm moving through water, I get to my feet and stroke his hair, feeling like I will collapse at any moment.

"Meghan, what are you doing?" he whispers. His lips look lifeless even in the warm light of the lamp.

"I love you, Brett. I don't want to kill you. I'm sorry, I'm so sorry I can't take your pain away. I can't do this. I love you. I'm just going to get some fresh air. I'll be back soon." I stumble to the door and unlock it. I have to get away from him before I can change my mind. I need to catch my breath.

He's calling me, but his voice is too weak for me to make out the words. I don't stop until I'm out of the house and running down the street under the hazy glow of the streetlamps. I'm running as fast as if I'm being chased, and my side quickly burns, but I don't care.

I would do anything for my husband, but not that.

CHAPTER 4

I don't stop running until I reach the far end of the street, where I collapse against a lamppost, gasping for air with my face pressed against the hard metal. A little while passes before I find the strength to lift my head and look up at the sky. It's cloudy, the slender moon shrouded by a thick veil of gray. I close my eyes and take in a deep breath before turning and making my way back to the house.

When I catch sight of Laurel standing in her garden and smoking a cigarette, I wonder if she saw me run down the street in my nightgown like a crazy woman. *Whatever*. I walk through the unlocked door but when I make it to the top of the stairs, my body grows weak again and I know I'm going to break down. I need more time before I see Brett in so much pain. I must be strong for him.

So I head down to the office, which always reminds me so much of him. I fling open the windows so the breeze can flood in, then I drop onto the leather couch, curling up into a fetal position and pressing my forehead against my knees as tears continue to flood my eyes. The pain in my heart is excruciating, but it's nothing compared to what Brett is going through. In my head, I can still hear his groans, raw and broken. The sounds of his suffering will forever be etched into my memories, and I can never erase them.

There's nothing I want more than to end his suffering, but I can't. I just can't. Not in the way he wants. I cry until I feel empty and exhausted, so much so that, despite myself, I fall asleep.

I awaken with a start from a vivid dream. In it, I got to my feet from this very office, and I climbed the stairs as if on the way to my own execution moments before helping my husband to die. Then I waited as the poison licked through his body like flames, and as he drew his final excruciating breaths, I wished I could take it all back.

When my eyes blink open in the dark, I'm so relieved it was a nightmare and nothing more.

"Thank God." I inhale sharply and cover my face with shaking hands.

When I lift them again, it hits me that I don't remember turning off the light before falling asleep. I must have been in such a state.

The time on the lit-up clock on the wall reads 12:30 a.m., but the clock has always been slow by twenty minutes. Brett kept saying he would fix it someday, but he never got around to it. Rubbing my aching head, I get to my feet, but I'm swaying as if I've had too much to drink. I walk slowly out of the office.

I can no longer hear Brett crying, not even in my head. The house feels eerily quiet, except for everyday sounds that have become familiar to the point that I often no longer hear them. The distant sound of the clock ticking, and the fridge humming as I walk past the kitchen door. Holding my breath, I climb the spiral staircase, counting each granite step to calm myself down as my hand glides over the cool wrought-iron railing. One. Two. Three.

Thirteen steps take me to the top of the staircase.

I pass Ashton's door. It's slightly open. In my broken state, I must have forgotten to close it fully. He has always preferred to have it open through the night, but now I don't like the idea of him listening to Brett's crying as it makes its way down the hall. For a moment, I stand outside Ashton's room, my hand on the door handle, then I close it.

I walk softly to the master bedroom and come to a halt again. I'm afraid to enter, to see my husband writhing in agony, and I'm ridden with guilt that I left him alone for so long.

A trickle of sweat trails its way down my left temple.

You can do this, I tell myself.

Until now, I have respected Brett's decision not to seek treatment, but I can't do it anymore. If he's still in so much pain, I will just have to call 911, whatever he says. At least in hospital they can give him some stronger painkillers and help to make him slightly more comfortable.

My palm is slippery against the metal handle, but it finally gives in and the door swings open. The room is the way I left it, of course, but something feels different somehow and I can't place my finger on it.

Brett is still in bed, but thankfully, the writhing has stopped. I'm relieved that he's sleeping now, but I also feel terribly guilty for leaving him alone when he needed me most. But I couldn't stay, I couldn't give him what he wanted. I needed to pull myself together, to think.

Then my gaze moves to the carpet and my blood runs cold. The syringe is next to the bed where I dropped it, but even from where I'm standing, I can see that it's empty.

My throat starts to close, and I stumble back.

He couldn't have. Did he find the strength to do it himself?

But he was so weak.

"Brett," I say, pushing the word through my throat in a strangled whisper. "Brett," I repeat when he doesn't respond. The sound of my voice is high-pitched and shrill now; it sounds unfamiliar and alien, echoing through the room.

My legs shake when I take a step forward, but I force them to move.

He's just sleeping.

He has to be.

I stumble to the bedside and crouch down next to him. With trembling hands, I reach out and brush his hair from his forehead.

His skin is cold. My breath catches and I gasp for air. I lean over him and press my ear to his chest. When I don't hear a heartbeat, I search for a pulse and find none.

No. He can't be. I clasp my hand to my mouth to stifle a scream, denial and horror battling in my mind.

What if, by some miracle, there's a pulse I can't find myself and the doctors can revive him?

My heart lodged inside my throat, I run to my side of the bed and grab my phone from my handbag, but when I try to press the numbers, it slides from my shaking hands. I snatch it up and dial 911, knowing that this is something I should have done hours ago.

The dispatcher promises that the paramedics will be at the house in fifteen minutes. In the meantime, I'm instructed to stay on the phone and to perform CPR. I turn on the speaker and try to bring my husband back, desperation consuming me, my every effort fruitless.

All the while I plead with him as my tears drip onto his face.

He doesn't answer.

He doesn't smile.

He doesn't blink.

He's not breathing.

It's too late. He's not coming back, the small voice inside my head taunts.

I refuse to listen to it.

I press my forehead against his and beg him not to leave me.

"Please, Brett, please don't do this to me. I need you. Ashton needs you. Baby, please open your eyes. Just give me a little more time; please don't go, not yet."

Silence.

I lie next to him and hold him tight.

When the paramedics arrive, I'm jolted to my senses and I grab the empty syringe and push it into a pocket in my handbag. If I had not filled it and brought it up for him, Brett would just be sleeping right now. It's all my fault.

The paramedics confirm my worst nightmare: Brett is gone. When they ask what happened, I tell them about his cancer and how he was in so much pain over the last few days, that he didn't want to go to hospital.

"I found him dead." Even though I'm telling the truth, my words sound hollow and unconvincing to my own ears, so I clear my throat and continue. "I came upstairs, and he was—" I break down then, and they can't get me to say anything more. More questions will come later, and I don't know if I'll be able to stop myself from telling them everything. How will I be able to think clearly when my heart and mind are shattered into a thousand pieces?

Brett's parents arrive while I watch his body being wheeled away. I don't even remember calling them. They sink onto the front steps and hold on to each other as they weep for their son. As soon as Brett's corpse is gone, I stumble into the house and head for the living room couch, dropping down onto it like a stone. My body is numb, but the fingertips that touched Brett's face just before he was taken away have a strange tingling sensation to them, and I hold them to my cheek. I want to cry, but it's as if I have no more tears left inside me.

I only sit for a minute before getting up again and heading to the stairs to check on Ashton, but at the bottom of the staircase someone grabs me by the wrist and spins me around.

"You did this," Nora hisses. "You killed my son."

I yank my arm from her grip and back away. I don't know what to say to her, because the truth is she is right: I prepared the poison and sucked it into the syringe. I brought it upstairs. I left it beside him.

"No, Nora." I shake my head slowly. "He was sick and—"

"You wanted him to die so you can take his money. That's why you talked him out of getting treatment. Tell me I'm wrong."

"You are wrong." I clench my jaw to keep from screaming at her. "For you to even think I could do such a thing is disgusting. My husband is dead. I'm grieving too; please just leave me alone."

Nora wipes the tears from her cheek with the back of her hand. "You won't be alone for long. I can assure you of that. Soon enough the cops will show up with questions. The truth will come to light, and you will pay for this, you piece of trash."

"Get the hell out," I shout. "I need you to leave now or—"

"Or you'll call the cops? They're already on their way. I called them."

"Mommy, what's happening?" Ashton's sleepy voice at the top of the stairs brings our argument to a screeching halt.

I throw Nora a warning look and move to take Ashton back to bed. "Grandma and Grandpa were just leaving, baby. Let me go and read you a story."

"Make it a good one," Nora says as I climb the stairs.

CHAPTER 5

Standing at Ashton's bedroom window after he falls asleep again, I'm unable to stop the tears that have finally arrived. They leak down my cheeks, one after the other, and after a while, the sobs come slower and quieter. I can't begin to process Brett's death, even though I've known it's been coming for months. It feels impossible to imagine a life without him, a world where he's no longer here.

When my eyes land on the police car parked in the driveway next to Nora's white Mercedes, I press my forehead against the glass and pull in a deep breath. I'm not ready to answer their questions, but I also can't stay up here and avoid them. I'm terrified of going downstairs, I feel safer in Ashton's room.

But if I delay, they might think I'm guilty.

Voices are floating upstairs now, and someone is calling my name again. Nora. She's still here, waiting to see me go down. I'm not surprised that she wants to be around when the cops question me.

I watch Ashton stir in his sleep and I pray he won't wake up before the cops leave, or to find that both his mom and dad are gone.

I feel physically ill as I close the door again and drag myself to the stairs. One of the cops is already making his way up, and I recognize him as Police Chief Robert Kane. He's a tall, heavyset man with graying mouse-brown hair, and his warm, green eyes and laugh lines don't fool me. I know whose side he's on. He's a friend of the Wiltons and, when I worked at the hotel, he used to be a regular in the hotel restaurant and bar. He was rude to the staff, always late for his reservations and demanding service as soon as he arrived, acting like he owned the place. His behavior might have been excused if he had at least tipped, but he never did.

I don't understand why the police are interrogating me, given that there hasn't been an autopsy that points to foul play. The only explanation is that the cops are doing this as a favor for the powerful Wilton family. Maybe they know this isn't my fault, but they're laying the groundwork for a custody battle that ends with me losing Ashton.

I can't bear the thought of them taking my child away, of losing yet another person I love.

"Good evening, Mrs. Wilton," the chief says. "I'm very sorry for your loss. Do you think you can answer some questions? I'm afraid it's routine."

I nod and wipe the tears from my cheeks. Even though I'm trembling inside, I do my best to pull myself together and steel myself for the barrage of questions. I follow the cop down the stairs, where Nora and Cole are now standing by the window, holding each other. Their eyes are fixed on me, and I sense they're trying to be intimidating, thinking that I'll mess up my story and set a trap for myself. Cole hasn't said a word to me since they arrived, but I'm sure he's also blaming me for Brett's death. It's evident in the way his eyes flash with anger when they meet mine, his lips pressed together into a thin line. I can almost feel him probing me, searching for guilt.

Another police officer is studying a multi-colored abstract painting on the wall, one of the many decorations in this house that do not appeal to my taste but which I was not allowed to change or replace.

Cole offers the chief of police a seat next to a glass-topped coffee table, and I lower myself into an armchair not far from where he's sitting. Part of me wants to weep again, but I just feel numb. The pain will return later, but for now I'm glad I can keep myself together. I need to be able to think clearly.

"Nora filled us in on what happened, but I would like to hear it from your perspective. You were here with Brett all evening, is that correct?"

I nod. "Yes. Me, our son, and Jane, our housekeeper."

Jane. I haven't thought about her since I tried to talk to her in the kitchen and she turned her back on me. No one was in the kitchen when I went to get the syringe, but is it possible that she was watching? I'm sure the cops will question her as well. To be honest, it's strange that even with all this commotion she hasn't left her room to see what's going on.

Before I answer, I look past the officer's shoulders at Nora. She's still standing by the window in her husband's arms, crying quietly as she waits for Chief Kane to break me with his questions. I used to think hate was a strong word, but nothing else can describe the crawling sensation I feel when my eyes meet the fury in hers. Part of me feels sorry for her, I can't imagine how painful it must be to lose your child. But I can never forgive her for casting blame on me for Brett's illness, for putting me through this torment when we should be comforting one another.

I can't believe this is happening.

I take a breath and tell the chief the same story I told the paramedics, painting those terrible hours that turned my life upside down. I tell them that after seeing Brett in so much pain, I left the room for a while, and when I returned, I found him dead.

"How could you? How could you leave my son to die alone and in pain," Nora interjects as she pulls away from Cole, who's trying to calm her down, assuring her that justice will be served, his eyes still on me. "She lied about loving my son," Nora continues. "She was only interested in his money. I... we visited Brett yesterday and while he was very unwell, he still had time. She just couldn't stand caring for him anymore and wanted to hasten his death."

I know I shouldn't care about what Nora thinks of me, but her words hurt, nonetheless. I wish she understood how much I loved her son. I wish she knew that I would have done anything to make him better and would have gladly died in his place.

Even though all that is true, I know that if ever Brett's plan and my role in it comes to light, I will be right in the center of a murder case. I will be called a murderer.

"Nora... Mrs. Wilton, if you don't mind, I would like to speak to your son's wife alone."

"I don't understand why that's necessary," Cole answers on Nora's behalf, his voice booming. "We might have some of the answers she's not giving you."

"I appreciate that, but we only need a few minutes."

Nora's eyes blaze at Chief Kane. At first, I think she's going to refuse to leave, but I sigh with relief when she clears her throat and walks out.

The chief turns back to me. "For how long was your husband sick?"

"He was diagnosed with cancer earlier this year."

Memories of that day flash back to me, that morning in the doctor's office when we learned about the diagnosis. I remember my body going limp, while my fingers curled tightly around the arms of the chair. I remember Brett staring down at the floor, his jaw clenched, his face ashen. On the drive home, the silence was so thick between us that it was unbearable, even with the radio playing. That same silence remained between us for a week. Brett did not want to talk about the cancer, and I didn't have the willpower to talk about anything else. It was all I could think about.

"And you say he refused treatment?"

"Yes. The doctors recommended chemotherapy, but he completely refused. I tried to convince him, but he wouldn't do it." I glance out of the floor-to-ceiling window toward the darkness outside. It must be close to 2 a.m.

Guided by the garden lights, my gaze follows the gravel path to the small fountain in the middle, where we would sit together, Brett and I, and talk about our future. The darkness beyond is impenetrable, like the hole that has just appeared in my life and my heart.

"He was in so much pain tonight," I murmur, then I glance back at the chief, who's still jotting down my words onto his notepad.

A heaviness settles in my chest, my eyes burning with unshed tears. I'm exhausted, and I wish they would all just leave me alone so I can go and sleep, and convince myself that this was just a dream. I'm not ready to face the harsh reality yet. I'm not ready to grieve for Brett because it's hard to accept that he's really gone, and he will never come back. But they're all still here, hovering around me, waiting for me to spill the truth, to confess, to prove them right.

"What was his prognosis?" the other officer asks. He's quite young, probably no older than twenty-five, but the police uniform makes him look older.

"The doctors gave him less than a year to live unless he had treatment."

"Do you know why he refused treatment?" Chief Kane asks.

"I saw on his computer that he'd researched stories of people who had chemotherapy and how horrible it was for them. He didn't want to go through that, especially if it ended up not working." I don't share with him that in his search history, I also found results for "the quickest ways to die".

"Was there any medication he was taking to manage the pain?" The younger officer's muscular arms are crossed and his narrowed eyes are focused at me, and I'm surprised at the complete lack of empathy I detect in his demeanor. He has a chubby baby face that makes it easy to imagine how he had looked as a little boy. My mind drifting with my tiredness, I think about Ashton and how he once said he wanted to be a policeman. I hope that if he ever is, he will show more kindness than this man.

I swallow. "He did have painkillers, but tonight he refused to take any."

"Why do you think that is?" Officer Kane frowns, his thick brows joining in the middle.

"I don't know. He just refused."

"And he also refused to go to the hospital?"

"Yes." I pinch the bridge of my nose, my head swimming. I'm desperate to be able to lie down, to shut everything out. "There was nothing I could do to help him."

The second officer comes to sit down on the couch as well and leans forward. I raise my gaze to meet his eyes. "You mentioned that you left the room for a while. How long was that exactly?"

I hold on to his gaze. "A couple of hours... I fell asleep in the office, but before that, I went out for some air."

"Why would you leave your husband when he's in so much pain?"

I bite into my lip for a moment as Nora's earlier words cut deep into me: "How could you leave my son to die alone and in pain?"

My guilt is like a suffocating blanket. As I struggle to breathe, I wish I could go back in time, to hold Brett's hand, to sit next to him, to do my best to soothe him. But I didn't. Despite my promise at the altar to be there for him in sickness and in health, I walked away when he needed me most.

I take a deep, ragged breath and shake my head. "Because I couldn't stand it. I couldn't stand seeing him in agony like that. I just needed a moment, to go out for a few minutes. I didn't mean to fall asleep." I pause. "He was my husband, and I simply could not cope with seeing him like that."

"That's understandable," Chief Kane says and I smile at him gratefully, my eyes filling up again.

The younger officer pushes himself to his feet and leaves the room.

"Mrs. Wilton, I know this is hard." I can hear in Officer Kane's voice that he means it, and I feel so grateful for the first ounce of compassion I've received.

"Thank you." He gives me a moment to catch my breath before he continues.

"You said you fell asleep in the office. Would you mind taking me there?"

I don't understand why it's important, but I don't resist.

The first thing I see when we enter the office are the papers spread out on the desk. Next to them lies a handful of notes in my handwriting with a crumpled tissue on top of them. Cole and Nora don't know this, but, since marrying Brett, I had been helping him out with the Black Oyster financial reports. I'm quite good with numbers, and during Brett's illness, I took on more of the chief financial officer tasks, so his father didn't think he was slacking.

But yesterday morning, I was also working on a business plan for the bakery I was planning to open one day. Now I can't help but feel that my dream is about to go up in smoke, just like my dream that I would grow old with the man I love.

"So, you were in here?" he asks, looking around him. "Were you sitting or standing?"

I throw him a confused look. "Does that matter?"

"Please answer the question."

Don't annoy him, I tell myself.

"I was lying on the couch." I point toward it and remember my tears dripping onto the wooden floor. "I was crying. That's partly why I left the room, I didn't want him to see me cry. I wanted to be strong for him, but at that moment, I couldn't be."

"How long have you been married to Mr. Wilton again?"

"Five years."

"And how did you meet?"

"I was employed at the Black Oyster Hotel. That's where I met him."

"Was he the one who hired you?"

"No, it was his father." My stomach churns when I think of the day that changed my life, the moment I accepted the position there. How could I have known that it would end like this?

A moment passes while Officer Kane writes down everything. Then he glances up again. "How long did you date before you got married?"

"Less than a year."

"Can you be more specific?"

Tears prick the back of my eyes like tiny, hot needles. "Around three months."

I can see that the officer is judging me, his eyebrows raising just a little.

"We were very much in love," I add weakly. Why does nobody believe our romance was real?

"Was your mother-in-law correct in saying you married Brett for his money?"

The urge to lash out is so strong it awakens cramps in my belly, but I straighten my shoulders and look him straight in the eye. "No, I did not marry my husband for his money. I loved him." I know what everyone must think. I was a maid, with nothing to my name. I must have come across as a gold digger to them, only after a comfortable life where I didn't have to worry about where next month's rent money was coming from. Of course, I was grateful for my change in fortune, but the most important thing in my life was always Brett, the kind man I fell in love with who swept me off my feet, made me laugh, believed in me. "If you think I killed him, why on earth would I do that? Why wouldn't I just wait for the illness to take him?"

"I'm not thinking anything right now, Mrs. Wilton." He scratches his chin. "I just need to have a complete picture. I truly am sorry for your loss."

"Thank you." I wrap my arms around myself, feeling the chill. I hadn't even noticed until now that I'm still wearing my nightgown.

He pushes his notebook into his breast pocket. "I think we have everything we need for now, but we might return if we come up with any more questions."

"I understand." My voice comes out strained, anxiety digging its claws into my spine and tiredness weighing me down. I feel like I have been awake for weeks.

I watch as Cole and Nora speak to the policemen outside, before they all finally drive away.

Feeling dizzy, I stumble up the stairs, but I'm overcome with emotion and suddenly it's as if I can't breathe. I collapse at the top, forcing myself to take a deep breath as sobs rack my body, my mind flashing with images of Brett. Brett in his wedding suit. Brett waking me up with a kiss and a cup of coffee. Brett with his arms around me as we cuddle up on the couch. Brett holding our baby boy the day he was born. Brett waving at me from his car whenever he left for work.

The sound of a door closing cuts through the fog, and I pull myself to my feet and walk down the corridor leading to Jane's room, trying not to look at the framed photos of Brett, Ashton, and me on the walls. When I reach her door, I take a deep breath and knock.

"Jane?" I whisper, but I don't get a response. Maybe the sound didn't come from her room after all. I knock again, more firmly this time. "Jane, it's me. Can I come in for a minute? Please."

The door swings open, and Jane is standing there, her expression calm, her eyes cool. She looks comfortable and relaxed in a plain, white oversized T-shirt and her long hair is loose around her shoulders in waves. "Can I help you with something, Mrs. Wilton?"

"I'm sorry to disturb you so late. I just needed to talk to someone." I bite my lip and swallow, wishing she would just bring me in for a hug, and be the friend she once was. "Brett... he died tonight."

"I'm sorry for your loss," she says and a flicker of empathy flashes in her eyes, but it's gone so quickly I wonder if it was even there in the first place.

Tears are sliding down my cheeks, but she doesn't react anymore, and I clear my throat and try to keep my voice level. "I just wanted to let you know before the rest of the town finds out."

"Thanks," she says and glances behind her. "I'm sorry, I should umm, I should get some sleep."

"Yeah, okay." I swallow hard, trying to stem the flow of tears from my eyes. "I'll see you in the morning, then."

She gives me a tight smile and closes the door on our friendship forever.

CHAPTER 6

"Ouch!" I wince as hot water pours onto my hand, missing the mug by inches, and I run to the sink and turn the cold tap on over my scalded skin. While I watch the water disappear into the drain, my eyes fill with tears again. Brett is dead. From now on, when I make a cup of tea or coffee, it will only be for me, and I won't ever scold him again for putting too much sugar in his drink.

It's seven in the morning now, and I feel lost and confused without him here. I haven't slept at all, wandering in and out of rooms before crashing on our closet floor with my face buried inside his shirts and sweaters in search of his scent.

I switch off the faucet and grab a towel from the marble counter as I glance at the door. Jane is normally the first person to be in the kitchen making breakfast, but not today, and I'm glad I haven't seen her yet. Just a few hours ago, she made it clear once and for all that our friendship is dead.

I know that, any moment now, Nora or Cole will return, maybe even bringing the police with them again. Before I face them and their accusations, I need to spend some time alone with Ashton. It will kill me, but I must tell him what happened.

As I'm on my way out of the kitchen, I notice a piece of paper tucked under the glass fruit bowl and a pen beside it. I pick it up and unfold it to find a message written in hastily scrawled letters.

Dear Mrs. Wilton,

This is my notice of resignation, effective immediately. I'm sure you will understand that it's for the best. I have already notified Mr. and Mrs. Wilton. Take care and good luck. I hope you get everything you deserve in life.

Bye for now.

Sincerely,

Jane Drew

As I read the note over again, I want to feel sad or disappointed, but in a strange way, I only feel relief. After how she reacted to my excruciating pain last night, I can't imagine us being around each other anymore. I'm not sure if she's left already, but I don't go to her room to check. I need to get Ashton out of the house. He's my priority right now.

My son opens his eyes as soon as I enter and draw the blinds, rubbing them with his fists the way he used to do as a baby. His curly hair looks shiny in the morning light.

"Morning, Superboy." He chose that name for himself, imagining himself as a superhero.

"Morning, Mommy."

"Ashton—" I sit down on the edge of his bed, pulling him into my arms "—there's something we need to talk about. But let's go out, okay? We'll drive around for a bit, and maybe we can have breakfast outside."

Ashton loves it when we drive around with no destination in mind. It's something that used to calm him a lot as a baby when he was upset, too. I hope it will work this time.

"Okay," he says, his eyes brightening. "Is Daddy coming too?"

I bite the inside of my cheek and look away for a moment. I can't break down in front of him.

I shake my head. "No, baby, he's not."

"Is he still sleeping?" he asks, his gray eyes narrowing slightly.

"Yes."

I help him get dressed quickly, and he runs out the door, giggling with excitement that bruises my heart.

Marjorie, Laurel's mother, is in her garden watering her daisies while her cane leans against the fence that separates our houses. She stops to stare as she always does, but she doesn't wave. Like her daughter, she never liked me. I'm guessing she wanted her daughter to marry into Brett's wealthy family, and I took that away from her.

I ignore her and help Ashton into the car. The moment we pull out of the driveway, my eye catches sight of a white Mercedes turning into our street. Nora's car.

"It's Grandma." Ashton hops up and down in his car seat. "Can she come with us?"

"No, she can't, not today, baby." I tighten my hands on the wheel. "This is our alone time." With that, I step hard on the accelerator, and we drive away in a squeal of tires.

CHAPTER 7

"Should we eat our breakfast in the park?" I ask Ashton, trying to keep my voice cheerful.

I would have taken him to a café or a diner, but it would be a nightmare if someone came up to me and Ashton to offer their condolences before I've even told him. In this small town, news travels fast. So, we picked up some pastries at a small bakery. Ashton loves the park, too, and I want him to be in a comfortable location when I tell him the news that will change his life forever.

"It's early for going to the park," Ashton replies. The delight in his voice is unmistakable.

"It is," I say, forcing the words through my throat. "It's nice to do different things, right?"

"Yes, like an adventure. You're the best mommy in the whole world."

Before today, my heart would have soared at those words. I love being a mom and giving my child all the happiness I can. But the best mom in the world does not make the kind of mistake I did. The mistake that killed his father before Ashton even got a chance to say goodbye. I didn't think he had the strength to use it, but I made it easy for him to end his life by leaving the full syringe within his reach. And I came so close to doing it myself.

"And you are the best son in the world." I smile at him in the mirror, and he giggles before turning to look out the window. We drive in silence for a while, and when we arrive, I'm glad that the park is deserted, as I expected it to be. All the other kids will be on their way to school.

"Did you sleep well last night?" I'm testing the waters, trying to figure out if he saw or heard anything. Ashton is a deep sleeper, but between the ambulance and the police, there was a lot of commotion in the house.

"It was fun. There were policemen in my dreams."

My stomach tightens. "It wasn't a dream," I say in a strained voice.

Ashton must not have heard me because he has moved on to another topic.

"Mommy, the swings are free," he shouts excitedly. "I want to go on them first."

I peer out the window. Apart from a gray-haired woman taking photos of the roses with a white poodle at her side, no one else is around.

"Okay, let's do it," I say. "Let's go."

It's hard trying to be brave for my son, but it's something I'll have to do for as long as I live. For the rest of my life, I'll be watching every word I say so he doesn't find out the truth about his father's death.

If the truth ever comes out, will he hate me for letting it happen and for lying to him?

"This is the best day ever." He laughs and claps his hands as I help him out of the car.

I freeze when his words reach my brain, and a blast of pain sears my chest. One day, he will look back on today and realize it was the worst. He will always remember the day he learned his father had passed away. Or perhaps he's too young and will forget as time passes. But he'll know that I remember, and he might ask me to awaken the memories for him, to bring him back to the most painful time in my life. I can already feel the sense of loss that will hit him when he's old enough to understand how his father died.

He dips his head to the side and looks up at me with a frown. "Is school closed?"

Preschool. I forgot to call in to tell them Ashton wouldn't be coming, and I'll have to call them shortly. But, then again, they probably already know about Brett by now.

"It's not closed, baby. I just wanted to spend some time with you today." I reach out my hand to him. "Come on, let's go."

The fresh scent of summer flowers meets us, and I hold Ashton's hand tight as we walk on pebbles toward the white metal gate. He's skipping happily beside me, and I hate that I'm about to kill his joy, possibly forever.

The handle of the gate is cool and opens with a gentle squeak as it allows us entry into the park. There are many varieties of flowers lining the perimeter—tulips, petunias, roses, and others that I don't recognize. The leaves rustle in the July morning breeze, and despite myself I can't help noticing how peaceful and calm it is here, without the usual sounds of children laughing and playing. Sometimes I come here just to sit and relax with a book under the oak trees as I watch Ashton play, but it's usually busy. The park bench right in the center, next to a white painted cup overflowing with deep-red roses, used to be a favorite place for Brett and me.

I won't be sitting there anymore. With Brett gone, my heart has been scooped right out of my chest. This place is just another reminder of his absence, of the unbearable reality that I will never see him again.

Instead of sand, most of the areas of the park are covered in soft artificial grass to cushion the children's falls. Once I tell

Ashton about his father, will he ever again find a soft place to land?

Ashton wants to go to the swings immediately, but I tell him to sit with me on one of the benches first. My heart in my throat, I pull him onto my lap and hold him tight, pressing my nose into the side of his face and breathing him in. He still smells of the citrus-scented shampoo from his bath yesterday.

"Mommy, you're pressing me too hard." He giggles as he tries to push me away.

"Sorry." I release him, but not completely. I wish I could hold him forever. I wish I could protect him from the world. I turn him to face me and stroke his hair, unable to control my emotions anymore.

"Why are you crying, Mommy?" He reaches forward and touches my cheek with the tips of his fingers, and the feeling is like butterfly wings against my skin.

"There's something I need to talk to you about."

"Stop crying, Mommy."

"Mommy is sad." I blink away the tears. "Baby, Daddy is gone."

I don't know if I'm doing it right. I have no idea how one explains death to a small child. He knew Brett was very sick, and once Brett was in so much pain during dinner that Ashton asked if he was going to die. I had no idea he knew what death was. I'll never forget the terrified look on his face when he sat there, waiting for our response. I can't even remember what we told him.

"Where did he go?" he asks, playing with the pastry bag.

"To heaven," I say without hesitation. I hope it's true, although I've never really been religious. The thought of Brett simply having evaporated away, no longer part of the universe at all, is not something I want to think about.

"He's never coming back?" His eyes are wide as they gaze into mine.

I shake my head and pull him into my embrace. He doesn't push me away this time. "He's not coming back, baby."

Several heavy moments pass as I hold Ashton to my chest and gaze up at the cloudless sky.

"What's going to happen now?" he finally asks. "Will we go and stay with him in heaven?"

I want to smile and cry at the same time. "No, not yet. We still have a lot to do on Earth. We can't see Daddy right now, but he will never leave us. He will remain in our hearts forever." I point at the clear expanse of blue above our heads. "I think he's up there, looking down on us and smiling just like the sun is right now. He would have loved this beautiful day."

"Is Daddy's pain gone now?" he asks, his voice quiet and fragile.

"Yes, it is."

"Okay. I want to play now," he says suddenly and slides off my lap as I sit there in shock. He doesn't even shed one tear. I wish I could get inside his head to see what he's thinking. Has he already come to terms with what he heard? Is he trying to escape the conversation because it hurts too much?

Ashton runs around the park with his arms outstretched. "I'm an angel," he shouts.

"You *are* an angel," I call back.

He is my angel. If anything is going to hold me together during the next couple of months and years without Brett, it's going to be him.

He occasionally comes back to hug me, especially when he sees me crying, then he goes right back to playing. He's so excited to be at the playground that the pastries don't even interest him.

After a while, I tell him we need to get back to the house. Hopefully, Nora has already left and isn't waiting for us to return. She did call my phone, but I didn't answer.

As I watch Ashton play, the idea comes to me clearly,

inevitably. We have to leave, now. I can't risk going to jail and leaving my son without either of his parents. I don't know where we will go, but we'll survive.

When Brett asked me to help him die, he told me that there's an envelope in the safe with my name on it. He said if things went wrong, I'd find everything to help me and Ashton escape. I'll go back to get it, then I'll pack our things and check into a hotel with Ashton for the next few days while I decide where to go next.

Once I buckle Ashton inside his car seat, I slide behind the wheel.

When I drive past the Black Oyster Hotel, the pain inside my chest flares. I'm looking forward to getting away from here, away from all the memories.

I hear the wail of sirens before I see the house, and I get close enough to see police cars parked outside and people everywhere. Every fiber in my body is telling me to run. Before anyone can spot me, I turn the car around and drive off.

I won't give them a chance to arrest me. The moment the handcuffs click around my wrists, I know Nora and Cole will take my son. They always get what they want.

But not this time. This is a fight I will never let them win.

CHAPTER 8

My head is pounding, and I'm at a roadside grocery store grabbing toiletries, cheap clothing, and just enough food to get us through the next day or two. Nora has already called me ten times, and I just stared down at the small screen and watched her name flashing until it disappeared. I drove first to an ATM to withdraw as much money as I could, and once I hit the daily limit, I walked into a bank and asked for a few thousand dollars. When the bank teller asked me to wait, saying that she needed to discuss something with her manager, panic gripped my throat and as soon as she disappeared to the back, I fled.

We've now been driving for hours now, and my heart is still racing.

"Do you need to go to the bathroom, sweetie?" I ask Ashton.

"Yes, Mommy. I need to pee," he says in a deflated voice.

I pay for our shopping before taking him to the restroom, and the beefy, bald cashier with his arms covered by snake tattoos looks me up and down.

"You're not from around here?" he asks, causing the toothpick on one side of his mouth to wiggle.

"No, I'm not," I lie as I hand him the cash while at the same time glancing up at the small camera that's mounted on the ceiling.

Next to me, Ashton starts shifting around and crossing his legs.

"Need anything else?" the man asks, his eyes never leaving my face.

I kick myself for not wearing a disguise. There's a TV on the wall, and right now it's playing a baseball game, but once the press gets wind of Brett's death, it will undoubtedly be the lead story on the local news stations. Especially now I've fled. I've read enough books and watched enough movies to know that it's not only the guilty who end up behind bars. All that matters is whether you have a good and expensive lawyer or not, and I cannot afford one.

We need to get the hell out of here.

"We just need to use the restroom." I take Ashton's hand and wrap my fingers around it, a hand Brett will never get to hold again.

The man jerks his head to one side. "It's that way, to your left."

"Thanks." I tighten my grip around Ashton's fingers and take him to the back.

As soon as we open the door, the stench of urine hits me like a punch to the stomach.

"Mommy, it's smelly." Ashton covers his nose.

"I know, baby, but we have no choice. We don't want you to pee in your pants, do we?"

I take a deep breath of the tainted air and lead him to the stall. The toilet is unflushed and toilet paper is hanging from the holder and pooling onto the dirty floor.

Ashton refuses to enter. "Mommy, I don't want to pee anymore. I want to use the toilet at home."

"Sweetie, we can't go home now. We need to use this

restroom, okay? Then we'll go on a great adventure." I draw him to me and hug him to hide my tears.

I finally convince him to use the toilet after I've cleaned it up the best I can, then we hurry out of the building and get back on the road.

I have no idea how long we'll be driving, or where we'll end up, but getting as far away from Fort Haven as possible feels like the right thing to do. I would have wanted to go to the morgue, to see Brett for the last time and to say goodbye, but now that's not an option. I know that if we stay, I'll end up losing Ashton as well.

During the drive, Ashton asks a lot of questions, but after an hour of me avoiding them he stops and stares out the window at the grassy hills and rolling fields. Occasionally a farm with cows in the distance breaks up the landscape. It's beautiful, but all I can think about is that Brett will never again see what we see.

After driving for a few more hours, we enter a small town as the light begins to fade, the sun sinking into a pool of blood on the horizon. I'm completely exhausted, and I feel safe enough to stop the car and check into a motel for the night at least. Eventually, we may need to leave the state completely, but for now, we can rest.

I find a motel on the outskirts with peeling paint, dingy windows, and a faded sign above the door that reads: "Winterhill Inn". It has a shabby appearance, but it's close to a major road out of town. The woman at the desk barely glances at me as I pay for the room. It's small with a stained carpet and a lumpy bed, but it's the best I can do for now.

Fifteen minutes later, I'm sitting on the bed, clutching a cup of bland coffee from the vending machine while Ashton is watching cartoons. My vision is so blurred with tiredness that I can barely see what's on the screen. I wish I had someone to call, someone who cares.

Today more than ever, I miss my parents. Their car hit a

patch of black ice all those years ago and they spun out of control, hitting a tree. At the time, my only other living family members were my mother's estranged sister, Roxy, a successful lawyer in New York, and their elderly mother. The last time I saw my aunt was at my grandmother's funeral. She's never really shown any interest in me.

I never truly recovered from losing my parents, retreating instead to a dark place inside myself and becoming painfully shy, finding it hard to make friends and socialize. I did make a few friends over the years but found it hard to really get close to people and let them in, until I met Jane and Denise and I thought we would be friends forever. Then their jealousy about my new life tore the fabric of our friendships to shreds.

During the five years of my marriage, I tried to make friends with the people in Brett's circle, but even though they never said it to my face, I know they all believed that I married Brett for his money. They secretly despised me; they never thought a woman who didn't come from money deserved to be his wife. Brett was my whole world, but I still felt lonely.

There were things I have never been brave enough to tell him or anyone else, and now he will never know.

When Ashton was born, he became my best friend, the connection between our souls stronger than I ever imagined possible. Now our relationship is threatened by the secret I will have to keep from him forever.

I have never felt more alone.

As I listen to cars outside driving by and blaring horns, I'm suddenly tempted to call the police and come clean about everything that happened, but I know it will go badly for me, particularly with Nora pulling the strings. I finally find the courage to listen to Nora's messages, and I immediately regret it. Every one of her words drips with poison.

"What the hell do you think you're doing?" she asks. "If you think you can kill my son and kidnap my grandson and get away with it, you're wrong. You will regret this."

I watch Ashton as he pushes his hand into a bag of chips.

What if what I'm doing is the wrong choice? What if it hurts him in the long run?

"You can run, Meghan, but I will find you," Nora continues. "You will pay for what you did."

I switch off the phone, I can't bear to hear her threats anymore.

I wish I could go back to the house to get the envelope Brett left behind. I imagine there are some passports and maybe money to help me and Ashton start over, and not only would they be invaluable to me, but they will also look very bad if the cops find them. But going back there is too much of a risk.

I feel terrified, and completely lost.

I thought I knew what loneliness was, but as it turns out, I had no idea. Now I do, and it's suffocating me.

I glance at the clock on the wall. It's five minutes after four, over seven hours after we left the house to go to the park. My gaze moves to the TV screen. I don't usually like it when Ashton watches too much TV, I'd rather he reads books, but right now I've never been more grateful for television. I never thought there would come a day when I didn't want to speak to my son, but I'm terrified of the questions he will ask and I feel completely drained of energy. I curl into a fetal position, hugging my middle with both my arms.

I'm not a criminal. I don't know how one goes about trying to disappear. I don't know how to stop myself from being caught.

I can't think straight, so I do the only thing I have the power to do: I sleep. My eyes are closing involuntarily, and my final thought as I drift away is that maybe sleep will help clear my head, so I can come up with a plan.

I don't know how long I've been sleeping, but the sound of the TV blaring wakes me up again. Ashton is still awake and eating his chips, so it can't have been for very long.

As soon as I move, he looks at me excitedly. "Mommy—" he points at the TV screen "—Jane is on TV."

Swallowing down the bile that's pushing its way up my throat, I act fast. I grab the remote from him and switch off the TV before he can hear what's being said. The headline that scrolled across the screen before I turned it off drives fear and pain into my stomach.

The Wiltons' housekeeper has alleged that Meghan Wilton murdered her husband.

"No!" Ashton shouts, trying to take back the remote. "I want to see Jane. She's famous. Let's watch, Mommy."

I can't even speak.

What did Jane say to the press?

"I'll be… I'll be right back." I get to my feet and stumble into the small bathroom, still clutching the remote. I lean against the door, my breath coming out in gasps.

Brett is dead and I'm wanted for his murder. My friend thinks I killed him.

I stare at my reflection in the mirror. My eyes are bloodshot and puffy, and I look as terrified as I feel. Splashing cold water on my face, I try to compose myself and look out of the bathroom window. In the car park, a twenty-something-year-old woman is lifting a baby stroller from the trunk of a car while a little boy stands by her side, sucking a lollipop. A happy mother, a happy child. I envy them for their carefree lives, while my world is spiraling out of control.

I expect that the police will think I killed Brett, especially since I'm clearly running. The search history about euthanasia will still be on his computer, the envelope in his safe will show that it was planned. But Jane?

A dark thought niggles at the back of my mind, and I cover my mouth with both hands.

What if I really did it?

When I woke up in the office, the lights were off, and I know they weren't when I went into the room. So did I get up and move around, but just can't remember it? I dreamed of injecting Brett with the poison. What if that was real?

And what if Jane saw it happen?

It wouldn't be the first time I sleepwalked. I did it often as a child and occasionally as an adult, especially when I was stressed. The last time I remember doing it was five years ago, the week after I married Brett, brought on by the weight of the secrets I kept from him. I had several more episodes after that, but they were few and far between.

Am I capable of killing my husband in my sleep?

Wrapping my arms around my middle, I shiver, debating whether I should tell the police what I suspect. But I can't. Nobody will ever believe I didn't kill him on purpose. And how could I even prove that I'm innocent, especially after disappearing for hours?

Trembling, I splash my face with cold water again. I don't bother to wipe it away this time, and it drips down onto my T-shirt.

It's over. My whole life has crashed and burned.

I lower myself onto the toilet, and pressing my head between my legs, I force myself to breathe. From a distance, Ashton calls my name, but I don't answer. I can't find my voice.

"Mommy, open the door," Ashton begs from the other side, rattling the door handle.

I wipe away the tears and force myself to get up. "I'm coming," I whisper.

I wish I was alone and could allow grief to break me apart. But I can't. For his sake, I need to force myself to function.

When I finally unlock and open the door again, Ashton is standing right there.

"Are you okay, Mommy?" He gazes up into my face, frowning a little.

It hurts to smile, but I try. "I was a bit sad."

He presses his small frame against my legs and attempts to wrap his arms around my body, reaching only up to my waist. "Don't cry, Mommy. Daddy is sleeping in heaven," he soothes, his voice muffled by my T-shirt.

More tears come, falling onto his head, the moisture tightening his curls, and I hold him until he pushes away again. Then I crouch down and hold his hands in mine. "You and I are going on another great adventure."

"Are we going camping?" His face lights up.

Ashton loves everything that has to do with the outdoors. The one time we went camping, he had the time of his life and didn't stop talking about it for weeks.

"No, not camping, but we're going far away. We will have so much fun together."

"I'm in." He raises his little hand for a high-five, and as my palm meets his, I promise myself that I will never let him down. I will keep him safe. I will do everything in my power to make sure he isn't taken away from me.

CHAPTER 9

ONE YEAR LATER

Willow Creek, a serene small town of only three thousand residents, is located in Tennessee close to the Great Smoky Mountains National Park. The idea to move here came to me in the motel that first night, when I was thinking about Jane's betrayal. This was her hometown. Even though after getting clean she did not want to return for a long time, she still had fond memories of it from her childhood. She had told me about the rural feel of the town, how her favorite thing to do was pick wildflowers in the open fields near the house she grew up in, and how it was the best place to get away from the city bustle. It always sounded so perfect.

When we first drove through, I was still undecided, but when I saw the breathtaking scenery with the river running through it and the mountains all around, I knew I didn't want to leave.

The residents of Willow Creek have no idea who I am, of course. They think of me as the crazy widow who lives in an old cabin in the woods with her son, whose new name is Clark. My new name is Zoe Roberts, but not many people call me that. "Crazy widow" is more interesting, I guess. Fine by me.

Ashton chose the name Clark for himself, like his favorite superhero, after I told him we were spies and needed new names to stay undercover. After using the name Clark for a while, he got used to it, and now I even call him Clark in my dreams.

Ruth Foster is one of the very few people here who see me as a normal person, and she has been a lifesaver. She is short and skinny with silver hair, big amber eyes, and wrinkled skin that's marked by liver spots. Her back is permanently hunched over from years of bending over her sewing machine, and she loves to wear long, colorful homemade dresses.

"You go and have yourself a good day," she says now with a bright smile as she reaches for Clark's hand. "I'll take good care of your little man."

"I know you will." My lips stretch into a smile, a small gift for the woman who has given us shelter for nine months. The old cabin we call home belongs to her, and she takes care of my son when I go to work. She even homeschools him, as she used to be a teacher. I'm grateful for that because enrolling Clark in a school right now is out of the question since he could say something to blow our cover, or someone might recognize him and alert the cops.

Ruth doesn't know who I am either, but she's not the curious type.

My decision to stay was confirmed the same day we arrived in the town, when I noticed a handwritten advertisement stuck to a cork noticeboard in a store, for someone to live in a nearby cabin. When I called the number and Ruth told me the tiny amount we would have to pay, it occurred to me that she was not renting because of the money. I figured that maybe she just needed someone to take care of the place. But as we got to know each other and she welcomed us into her world, I realized that she might have wanted company as well.

The cabin in the woods is very much in need of repair, but

it has a rustic and cozy feel, as well as big windows that let in natural light and a beautiful view of the mountains. I fell in love with the place immediately, from the large cherry tree out front to the privacy it offered.

Before I knew it, days had morphed into weeks and weeks into months and now almost a year has gone by, and we're still here. My little boy has stolen Ruth's heart, and she has given us permission to stay for as long as we like. She told me that the cabin once belonged to her late husband, Jacob, who escaped to it a few times a week for some peace and quiet.

When Ruth offered to care for Clark, I was hesitant at first, but she insisted, and I did need her help. As a young woman, she'd founded the first kindergarten in town, and she said that seeing kids every day lit up her life.

"I'll pick him up at eight." I ruffle Clark's hair.

One thing I've learned while being on the run is that I need to try and keep every single one of my promises. I want to keep on everyone's good side. I go where I'm going and come back when I say I will. I don't visit unnecessary places. I go to work, I buy groceries, and I keep to myself.

I step away from the door and wave at them as I walk to my second-hand Chevy hatchback. To prevent the cops from tracking me down, I bought it shortly after leaving Asheville at a ridiculously low price because it was a clunker and had been sitting in a local dealership lot for weeks.

It's been a year, and I have not been found, but it doesn't get any easier. Every day I keep waiting for the cops to arrest me or for Nora and Cole to show up.

I can never forget Nora's last words to me.

You can run, Meghan, but I will find you.

Finding a job as a newcomer in a close-knit town was tough, but Ruth helped get me a waitressing job at the Lemon Café &

Restaurant, which belongs to her acquaintance, Tasha Lake. Like the fruit it's named after, Lemon (as the locals call it) has a bright-yellow exterior and round tables with striped yellow and white tablecloths. Even the air inside is lemon-scented with essential oils and candles. Today there are only a handful of regulars occupying the tables. They glance at me briefly before returning to the pork chops and potato salad lunch special, along with the signature fresh mint lemonade that's always on the menu.

A part of me is always expecting to find Nora sitting at one of the tables.

The days are long and with July being the hottest month of the year, the heat is unbearable. There isn't even much of a breeze coming through the open windows, but soon the lunch special displayed on the chalkboard outside the restaurant draws in more people than usual. Normally, a rush is my cue to help out in the kitchen for a while.

Two months ago, Raphael, the head chef, suffered a terrible migraine and had to leave work early. Since there was no one to replace him, and the guests were demanding their food, I asked to step in. My cooking skills impressed everyone to the point that I now work with one foot in the kitchen and the other in the dining room. I prefer it that way. When my anxiety takes over and I become paranoid about Nora or the police walking in, I can retreat to the kitchen, and I always aim to do more than what's expected of me.

But I can't hide in the kitchen today. We only have three waitstaff instead of the usual four and the kitchen is fully staffed.

"You are a godsend, you know that?" Tasha comes to stand next to me as the lunch guests finally start trickling out, and we have a moment to catch our breaths.

"What do you mean?" I wipe the sweat off my brow with a napkin.

"You seriously don't know?" She raises an eyebrow.

Tasha is a year younger than me, with dark-brown skin and equally dark hair in twists that are always piled up in a messy bun on top of her head when she's working. In her long, flowing skirts, melon-colored tops, and the lemon earrings she's so fond of, she fits right in with the feel of her restaurant.

The Lemon is Tasha's pride and joy that she built from the ground up. Before I came along, she ran it with her brother until he left to open his own club.

"I really don't know what you're talking about, Tasha. I'm just doing my job." I grab a rag to go and wipe down the table of the last guests to leave.

She follows me, arranging the chairs while I wipe away crumbs and gravy.

"You are a really hard worker. Do you ever take a moment to breathe?"

Breathe? Sometimes it feels like I haven't really breathed normally since I came into that room and found my husband dead. But, of course, she doesn't know that.

"I love this job, and you pay me to do it." My pay is not much, but it's enough to pay the rent and buy groceries. I always put the tips in a savings jar at home, for a day when my son and I might once again have to be on the move. "I'm grateful for the work."

"Tasha, Zoe, see you tomorrow."

We turn to wave at Sandy, another waitress. She studies at the University of Tennessee in Knoxville and works at Lemon whenever she's in town.

"I guess I'm telling you that I appreciate having you as an employee. Sometimes, I wonder what I would do without you."

"Whatever you did before me." I smile. "This place was a huge success before I came along."

"Trust me, before you came along, we could barely hold our heads above water." She touches my arm. "You really do a lot here, but I want you to take some time off to get some rest and spend time with your son."

"I do take some weekends off."

"I know, but you still come in sometimes when we're short-staffed."

"I'm happy to do it." I don't tell her that working hard keeps me from thinking too much, and every tip I get from a customer makes a difference.

"I'm glad." Tasha squeezes my arm. "But if you ever need a couple of days off, please let me know. I already feel guilty as it is. And as your boss, I insist that you take a short break now before the dinner guests arrive." She stretches out her hand for the rag. "We could have coffee together if you like."

"Yeah, that would be nice."

I know Tasha wants us to be friends. She always takes time out of her day to chat with me, and three times now she has invited Clark and me to her house to have dinner with her, her husband, and their twin boys. I always decline. I would so dearly love a friend, and I really like her. An occasional coffee with Tasha at the restaurant when things are slow is lovely, but being a recluse is safer for Clark and me. I can't afford to get close to anyone, not when there's a chance I could blow my cover.

The news of Brett's supposed murder was so big that it reached Willow Creek, and not long after I arrived, my face was still in the newspapers with the word "wanted" in the head-lines. Of course, I have done my best to disguise my appearance with a new hair color and cut, and glasses I don't need. Now things have died down, but I still need to keep my guard up.

After our break, a man with black jeans and a leather jacket struts in, and we stop what we're doing to stare. He has a square face, a well-formed nose, full lips, and perfectly shaped eyebrows above moss-green eyes. We're not the only ones staring at him. Eva, the youngest waitress, is practically drooling. She was watering the plant near the restaurant entrance, but now the water can is neglected at her feet.

Tasha leans into me and whispers. "If I weren't married to my dream man, I'd gladly commit a crime just so he can arrest me."

"He's a police officer?" I instantly snap back to reality.

"Brand spanking new in town. He's probably off-duty, hence the lack of uniform. Apparently, he's been working for the WCPD for a week or two now, but it's his first time dropping by." She gives me a small shove. "You should go and get his order."

"I... no." My heart is starting to race. "I was going to ask Raphael if he needs a hand with dinner preparations."

"No need, he has everything under control. Go and help that gorgeous man, and make him feel very welcome, my dear." Tasha winks. "I have some paperwork to do in the office. Call me when more guests arrive and you need a hand."

I swallow hard. "Okay."

With trembling hands, I take my notebook and a pen, push back my shoulders, and head to his table. He's already flipping through the menu.

He looks up with a smile. "Hey there."

"Hi, welcome to Lemon." My voice is as cheery as expected of me, and my pen is hovering over my notebook. "What can I get you?"

"How about a big glass of vodka?" His eyes crinkle at the corners as he grins.

"I... sorry, umm, we don't have vodka. Is there anything else I can offer you?"

"I'm kidding." He chuckles. "I'm about to start my shift, so no alcohol for me."

"Okay then," I say and wait for his real order.

"Let me see." He lowers his gaze back to the laminated menu. "Please bring me a fish burger with lots of hot sauce and a large Coke," he says, smiling up at me.

"Of course. I'll be right back with your drink."

I can feel his gaze following me to the front of the restaurant. Is he wondering why I look so nervous? Does it show from the outside?

When I return to his table with his drink chilling my palm, my knees are so wobbly I can barely walk.

"I haven't seen you around yet." He lifts the drink to his lips, the ice clinking in the glass. "I've only been in Willow Creek for a few weeks. So, what's your name?" he asks.

"Zoe," I murmur.

"Zoe," he repeats. "It's a pleasure to meet you." He stretches out his hand.

I glance past him and notice Tasha watching us from the kitchen entrance, a smirk on her face. She's clearly pleased.

"Nice to meet you." I shake his hand quickly.

"I'm Officer Roland, but you can call me Tim."

"Okay." I don't want to call him anything at all. I want to serve him his food and then never speak to him again.

"I'll bring your meal." I turn on my heel and navigate mechanically around the crowded tables toward the kitchen, uncharacteristically ignoring at least one customer as they try to get my attention.

Tasha hurries to me. "Is he as good-looking close up? I think he likes you. He actually has his eyes on you right now."

"It doesn't matter. I'm not interested."

"But Zoe, it's been over a year since your husband died. I know it must be hard, but don't you want to date again one day?"

"I'm not ready." I swallow hard.

Tasha tries to get me to open up some more, but I don't lower the wall between us. Eventually she gives up and I throw myself into the lunch service, glad for the distraction. I don't speak to Officer Roland again until he leaves, giving me a tip larger than the amount he spent on his food. I try to give some of the money back, but he refuses.

At the end of my shift, I drive to Ruth's to pick up Clark, but panic bubbles up inside my chest when I don't find them at the house.

Ruth is not answering her phone, either.

I drive around town frantically, and as the minutes go by, I'm close to going crazy with worry when she finally returns my call. They're back at the house.

When I get there, Clark runs into my arms. "Hello, Mommy."

I'm still shaking as I pull him close.

"Good evening, Zoe," Ruth says. "Clark was such a good boy that I promised him ice cream after dinner."

I shut my eyes, trying hard to control my emotions. I can't lash out at Ruth. I need her, and in a normal world, she did nothing wrong. She cares about my son and just wanted to give him a treat.

"Thank you," I say, my voice trembling. "But next time, please let me know if you want to take Clark out."

"I didn't think you would mind."

"I... I worry, that's all."

She clasps her hands in front of her. "I understand. It won't happen again."

I nod and force a smile. "Thank you again for your help."

Losing my son is my worst nightmare. And while I know all too well that the worst of dreams can come true, I pray that this one won't.

CHAPTER 10

I'm kneeling next to the bed, watching Brett's face contort into a grimace as his hands claw at the sheets until they're in his fists. The pain is only increasing, twisting his features until they are unrecognizable.

When the pain finally gives him a break, he opens his eyes and pleads with me to help him, his lips only able to say one word. "Please..."

I can feel the blood pounding in my temples so loudly, it's almost deafening. I put both my hands on the covers over his chest and can feel how damp they are, soaked through with his sweat. I stare down at the man I love, my mind trying to process the impossible. It feels like the world has stopped.

Tears roll down my cheeks and I press a hand to his drenched forehead.

"I can't. Baby, please, don't ask me to do it."

I can't kill my husband. I can't. But my gaze moves to the full syringe on the nightstand, and when he starts crying, I pick it up, holding it in the palm of my hand.

"Please," he mumbles again, his words coming slower. "If you love me—"

"I do. You know I do." Trying not to think, I watch as my shaking hand brings the syringe to my husband's arm, his muscles clenching and unclenching as he tries to fight off the pain, the pain he wants me to stop. As if my hand is detached from my body, I watch it pressing the long, thin needle against his skin and pushing the plunger, allowing the poison to enter his body.

But before he dies, someone talks to me. It's Clark.

"Wake up, Mommy," he calls, touching my cheek.

We sleep in the same bed, because I never want to be apart from him. I don't want to wake up one day to find him gone.

"Mommy, you were crying in your sleep again." His voice is still sleepy.

"I'm so sorry, baby." I wipe the sweat from my forehead and pull him into my arms. "I had a bad dream."

"Don't be scared," he says. "It's not real."

I bury my head into his little body, hating that I wake him with my night terrors. I hope he's right, that the dream was not real.

Once he's fallen back to sleep, I take a Xanax to calm me down. But it's still a while before my heart stops racing. The last time I had this dream was a month or so ago, and not for the first time I can't help wondering if I'm responsible for Brett's death and my mind blocked it out. As I have done so many times before, I squash the thought before it pulls me under, and gradually fall back into a fitful sleep.

A few hours later, I look out of the window toward the mountains, lit up by the newly risen sun, and the pink and yellow paint strokes across the sky. It's Sunday, a beautiful morning, and I have the day off.

"Go brush your teeth," I say to my yawning son. "We're

going to have a special day today. How about we bake some cupcakes for Mrs. Foster?"

Baking has always been my escape, bringing me a sense of comfort that most things can't. I love that it gives me the power to take something bland and make it delicious, to create beauty even when life turns ugly. It also reminds me of my mother, who was a fantastic baker. I clearly remember the smell of her freshly baked cinnamon buns wafting down the hallways and leading me to the kitchen where the marble counter would so often be topped with goodies like blueberry muffins, chocolate chip cookies, pumpkin pies, and cupcakes covered in butter-cream frosting. Climbing up on the cream, granite kitchen counter, I would wrap my arms around her soft, warm body and breathe in the sweet scent of her skin. I love to bake for my son so I can pass on some of those memories to him, in an attempt to make him feel safe and loved.

Even though I love to bake, I don't have much of a sweet tooth. I taste what I bake only to see if I'm headed in the right direction, but I never really love the final product. I just bake for other people, and sometimes I bake at Lemon. When I bake, I can convince myself that I'm not as useless as I often think I am, and I feel less alone, like my mother is back here with me.

Creating something from nothing gives me a sense of purpose, but the good feelings only last until the oven is switched off, the flour is wiped off the counter, and the baking tools are put away.

Clark loves to watch me bake and I'm glad that in these moments, his little mind is focused on something other than the dark memories of his father's death. He doesn't talk about it often, but I know he misses his dad.

"What kind of cupcakes should we bake?" I ask him after my shower.

"Mrs. Foster likes chocolate. You know that, Mommy."

"You're right. Sorry, I forgot."

The bright-white kitchen sports a country charm with shiplap walls, exposed ceiling beams, open shelving, and a huge apothecary cabinet with brass handles that serves as an island, a kitchen table, and storage space all in one. The collection of hanging copper pots and bright-orange curtains break up the white and bring a touch of warmth and life to the otherwise sterile space.

Whenever I'm inside the kitchen, I feel like I can escape to another time and place and pretend my problems don't exist.

I stand in front of the cream Aga stove and reach into the shelves above it for the baking ingredients. The Terracotta crock where I keep the flour is empty, so I go into the tiny pantry at the opposite end of the room. I gather everything I need from the pantry and get out before I become claustrophobic. Some people might find my fear of being trapped inside small spaces ridiculous, but it's a fear I'd had since I was a child, and I haven't ever managed to shake it off.

Soon, the kitchen is transformed into our own personal bakery. When I pour the flour into a bowl, flower dust floats upward into my face, and Clark laughs. For a split second, I allow myself to join him. I don't often feel joy so freely anymore, but this moment is ours alone. We don't get to go out much, but we get to do this.

Clark helps me stir the cupcake mixture and fill the baking tray, and once the cupcakes are in the oven and I'm cleaning up, he gets his coloring book to make the time go faster. When the aromas of chocolate, lemon zest, and vanilla swirl around the room, he helps me decorate the cupcakes with buttercream, lemon slices, and mint leaves.

Now that we've finished baking, dread wraps itself around me. I know it's just because of that awful dream, but I can't help feeling that something bad is about to happen. It's the same feeling I had the night Brett died, seconds before I found him in our room.

We drive the cupcakes over to Ruth, who lives twenty minutes away, and we find her sitting out on the porch, knitting something that looks like a scarf. She says it's for Clark and puts it away quickly.

I'm touched, but I wonder if Clark will ever wear it. Will we still be in Willow Creek when winter comes around?

"Is that for me?" Ruth asks, pointing at the tray in Clark's hands.

"They're cupcakes!" Clark says before I can answer.

"Did you make them, Clark?" She smiles brightly.

"I helped Mommy."

"You are one talented boy." She takes one of them from the tray and bites into it. "Delicious as usual." She raises her gaze to mine. "Have you thought more about what I said?" she asks.

She has been telling me often to open my own bakery, after I told her once that it had been a dream of mine. She said life is too short to hold back on pursuing our dreams.

"Yes." I pull my gaze from hers. If only she knew how complicated it is for me. "Maybe someday I will."

I'm relieved when she goes back to chatting with Clark, telling him stories of her childhood, as if he were her own grandchild.

"Well, we have to go now, Ruth. It was lovely to see you," I say after the third story.

"Why don't you leave Clark with me? He can keep me company."

"I'd love to, but I promised him another ice cream because he was so good in the kitchen today." The truth is, I also want to spend time with my son.

"Well, in that case, off you go, young man." Ruth ruffles Clark's hair and he slides down off the porch swing. When we get back into the car, she gives us a small wave and returns to her knitting, the tray of cupcakes next to her.

Although Clark would have loved to sit at an ice cream shop, I can't risk being out in public for too long, not when we can avoid it. So we drive to the grocery store to pick up a tub of his favorite chocolate and caramel ice cream.

I'm about to pay when my body senses a strong presence behind me, a tingling sensation as if I'm being watched. I spin around and scan the faces behind me, but there are none that I recognize, and no one comes across as suspicious. Still feeling uneasy, I pay for the ice cream and grab Clark's hand.

Inside the car, Clark wants to start eating the ice cream right away. I tell him he can't because he doesn't have a spoon, but he insists on using his finger. Usually, I stand my ground, but I don't have the energy right now. I feel shaken and on edge, and I'm just desperate to get back to our cabin. I give him the tub of ice cream and he digs into it, licking his fingers with glee.

By the time we get home, my stomach is in knots. Full of anxious energy, I walk around, making sure everything is in its place, checking the door is locked behind us and the oven is off. But inside the kitchen, dread creeps up my spine.

One of the two cupcakes we left behind is missing.

I call Clark and he comes running. "Did you eat one of the cupcakes?" I ask him.

"No." He shakes his head.

"I left a cupcake each for us, remember?"

He eyes the cupcake on the table and shakes his head again. "No, Mommy, I think you only left one."

I'm certain I left two.

"Sweetie," I say, turning him to face me, "did you just forget? It's okay to tell Mommy if you don't remember."

"I didn't forget." He stomps one of his feet. "I'm not lying, Mommy. I'm not."

"Of course not, baby. Of course not." Feeling terrible, I pull him to me and kiss the top of his head.

A moment later, he leaves me standing in the kitchen, wondering whether I'm finally losing my mind.

CHAPTER 11

As soon as Clark falls asleep, I put away the book I was reading to him and tiptoe out of the room, closing the door softly. The newspaper articles I printed out at the restaurant today are sitting in the living room. I don't own a laptop because I can't afford one, and there's no internet connection in the cabin. Not that I'd want to go online much, anyway. I'm too paranoid about being tracked down.

Tasha gives me permission to use the computer in her office whenever I want, but I'm always nervous that I might leave behind some clues about who I am. So I only use it quickly once a month, and I always make sure to delete my history after I'm done.

I spread out the articles related to Brett's murder and brace myself before picking up the first one. It's an article I already read, so I sift through the papers to find a more recent one.

I find one that's only two days old, and my breath catches in my throat as I read it.

They haven't given up. They're still searching for me.

My fingers stroke the birthmark on my collarbone as I look at the photograph staring back at me. That mark is the one thing

I cannot change about my appearance, but I keep it well hidden underneath clothing and makeup.

The paper trembles in my hand as a I read, and I try to breathe slowly and keep myself calm. I scan the article, reading every word slowly and imprinting it in my mind.

> *Meghan Wilton is wanted for the murder of her husband Brett Wilton, whose parents are offering a reward of $20,000 to anyone who informs them of their daughter-in-law's whereabouts. They refuse to give up hope that she will be found and brought to justice, and long to be reunited with their only grandson.*
>
> *Brett, a talented businessman, died mysteriously on July 20 last year, and his death shook the small town of Fort Haven. The couple's housekeeper, Jane Drew, said she saw Meghan filling a syringe and taking it to their bedroom that night. She also claimed that she heard Brett, who had terminal cancer, sobbing and pleading for his life. Soon after, an autopsy concluded that Brett had died from a lethal dose of cyanide.*
>
> *After she was questioned by police, Meghan disappeared from Fort Haven with her son Ashton and has not been seen since.*
>
> *If you have any information pertaining to her whereabouts, we urge you to contact the police as soon as possible.*
>
> *The new police chief of Fort Haven has vowed to find Brett Wilton's murderer after Robert Kane, the previous chief of police, died in a car accident two months ago.*

The paper flutters to the carpet. I didn't know about the reward, but I had already heard about Jane's account of the events that night. I'm still struggling to come to terms with it; it's hard to understand how my old friend could betray me like that.

But even worse, this is the first time I'm hearing about the substance that killed my husband. As I wipe away tears, I wonder if he was in even more pain before he died. Was it a quick death?

Did he die alone, or was Jane telling the truth?

Was I there, in my sleep?

Did I watch my husband die?

I had dared to hope that the case was running cold. But then again, I never really expected Nora to give up. I've managed to hide for a year, but now that there's a reward on my head it feels as though I'm reaching the end.

I stare at the piece of paper at my feet, then, without thinking, I snatch up the page and tear it to shreds. The pieces of paper fall on the floor, like the broken pieces of my life that I can't seem to put back together.

I want to scream out, but I don't want Clark to hear me. So, I rush out onto the porch, my fingers pressed hard against my throbbing temples, my teeth grinding against each other as I replay every word I read in my mind.

Whistling through the trees, the wind sounds like it's whispering the word *murderer* over and over. Nausea rolls in my stomach and I curl my hands into fists, desperate to shut out the sounds. But they only grow louder, spiraling out of control, a hurricane with me in the center.

"*Murderer, murderer, murderer*"

What do I do? Do I run again? And if I do, where would I go?

This cabin has protected Clark and me for a long time now. The thought of starting over in another town without anyone's help terrifies me. I close my eyes and take a deep breath, filling my lungs with as much air as possible, but my chest feels as though it's being crushed by a vice, the pressure of my heart punching against it almost too painful to bear.

Calm down. Calm down and think.

I cannot allow myself to come apart. I have Clark to think about.

There's only one thing for me to do right now. I need to lie low for a few days and stay out of the public eye. Being seen anywhere right now is dangerous.

I lower myself onto the porch swing and put my head into my hands for a moment before it snaps up again.

I don't know if it's my paranoia, but I feel as though I'm being watched.

I search the darkness and find nothing but shadows that dance like ghosts as the wind blows, and the flicker of fireflies. The creak of the trees and the sounds of small animals skittering through the underbrush creep me out, so I go back into the cabin and lock the door.

I walk softly around the cabin, making sure every single window is closed. Then I go to the bathroom and fetch one of the hair color boxes stacked inside the cabinet. It's time to touch up my roots. When I left Fort Haven, I was a long-haired brunette; now I'm blonde. It's vital that I don't look like my former self. I wear glasses too, and darker shades of clothing, hoping to fade into the background.

Tasha, who loves color, sometimes urges me to wear something with "a little more flash". She thinks I wear dark clothes because I'm still in mourning, and I know she just wants me to feel able to move on with my life. I do wish I could move on, but the past is always going to be running after me.

I've become such an expert at coloring my hair that it doesn't take long. Blonde hair makes me look pale and washed out, but I don't care. I've lost weight, too, and with my hollowed cheeks and glasses, an untrained eye would never recognize that the woman pictured in the articles is the same one who walks the streets of Willow Creek.

The next few days following that article will be critical; we will have to be more careful than we have ever been before. The good thing about Clark is that he has changed so much in the past year. He looked so small in the photos that were circulated on the news and by the police. But no matter what, I would never change my son's appearance. I don't want him to develop a complex, to think that I don't love him the way he is. But sometimes if we're going into really busy public places, I tell him to put up his hood or wear his sunglasses, reminding him that we are undercover.

As soon as I enter our room, Clark coughs and I freeze in the doorway. I hold my breath, expecting him to go back to sleep after stretching out a bit, but he doesn't. Instead, he sits up in the dark and calls for me. Kicking myself for being too loud, I head over to him and switch on the nightlight on my side.

"Sweetie, why are you not sleeping?"

"I heard sounds." He rubs his eyes with his fists.

"What sounds?" I frown and glance at the window.

"I don't know." He shrugs and looks at me. "Mommy, you look different."

"You need to go to sleep, Superboy. Should I read you another story?"

"No, Mommy." He draws closer to me on the bed, which is nestled between two bookshelves. "Can you make up one?"

I don't know how I will be able to make up a child's story with my head filled with fear. But to my surprise, I manage, and by the time I'm done, Clark is sleeping again.

I switch off the light, but I can't sleep.

My senses on high alert, I hear a dog barking from a distance, and the fast-flowing river that rushes past the cabin. The loudest sound is my heart thudding inside my chest.

I lie down on my pillow and try to still my thoughts, but, after a while, something slips into my mind and makes me sit up again.

All this time, I've been shifting between Brett killing himself somehow, despite his weakness, and me doing it in my sleep.

But what if I'm wrong about both? Could someone else have done it?

I press my fingertips to my eyes as I take myself back to that night.

I see myself walking back to the house after running off into the night. Laurel was outside smoking a cigarette.

Could she have gone into our house while I was away? The door was open. She did see how much Brett was suffering that day when she brought flowers, and she said to me that I couldn't keep her from seeing him. Could Brett have asked her to do the same thing he asked me, and she agreed?

And now, is she letting me go down for it?

After forcing myself to revisit that night, I'm more certain than ever that Brett did not kill himself. He was just too weak and in too much pain to pick up the syringe from the floor and inject the poison into his veins.

My gut is also telling me that I didn't do it. I couldn't bring myself to kill him when I was awake, and I can't imagine I would have done it in my sleep.

But I can't go to the cops. Maybe if I didn't have Clark to care for, I would try. But if I fail, I could lose my son. I can't let that happen.

CHAPTER 12

I sent Tasha a text message last night before I fell asleep, telling her I needed a few days off. I'm still shaken by that article, and by my realization that someone else could have killed Brett and they're trying to frame me.

Could it really be Laurel? She always hated me, and I know she loved him. She would have hated to see him suffer. Did she have the strength to do what I could not?

Tasha calls me first thing in the morning.

"Sorry I didn't get back to you last night," she says. "Is everything all right?"

"Not really." I glance at Clark, who's playing at the kitchen table with a LEGO set he got from Ruth. "I'm not feeling well. I was hoping you could manage without me."

"I'm really sorry. I want to give you today and tomorrow off, but there's so much going on. It's just not a good time right now, I really need you for the next two days. Sandy is going to a funeral, and we have two birthday parties. We might also need you in the kitchen. I promise you that after things calm down, you can take a couple weeks off."

My heart sinks. I have two options: I can refuse to go to

work and maybe lose my job, or I can go and hope nobody recognizes me from that article.

"I don't know, Tasha. I—"

"How about you come in for only two or three hours today? Please, Zoe. I need you. We are really short-staffed."

I squeeze my eyes shut and tighten my hand around the phone. Tasha has always been good to me, and I feel terrible for even thinking of letting her down. And I do need the money, especially the tips.

Maybe it will be fine.

"Okay." I sigh. "I can do that. I'll be there within the hour."

Ruth is pleased, at least. I already told her I had the day off, and she had sounded disappointed because she's so used to seeing Clark almost every day during the week. When I call to tell her that my plans have changed and he will be going to her after all, she's unable to hide her delight.

But Clark's little face crumples when I tell him I have to go.

"But you promised to stay with me today. We were going to make cookies."

"I'm sorry, baby, but Tasha needs me to come in. And you always have so much fun with Mrs. Foster. I'm sure she'll be very happy to see you."

Clark is in a terrible mood as I get him ready.

"You need to make it up to me," he says on the way to drop him off. He's heard that from me countless times recently, after the many times I've disappointed him.

"Yes." I'm relieved he's talking to me again. "How should I do that?"

"Ice cream," he says, and I shake my head.

"You've had too much ice cream the past few days."

"But Mommy, you owe me."

I can't help but laugh. "How about something else? I could buy you a new book or a puzzle."

"Okay, I'll think about it," he says, and I smile, shaking my head.

When we arrive at Ruth's house, she's already waiting for Clark on the porch.

She lives in a quiet, middle-class neighborhood in a two-story house that Clark says reminds him of a house from a fairy tale. The Victorian-style structure with its maroon door is decorated with white delicate lace-like trim, and there is a wrap-around porch with wicker furniture to match the door and plump white cushions.

The potted plants on either side of the porch entrance are overflowing with white and pink roses, and flowering bushes. Today, Ruth is wearing a loose, red and white polka dot dress, and she fits right into her perfect home.

I hand my son over and she gives him a hug. Clark has finally cheered up and now he's looking forward to spending the day with his adopted grandmother.

I watch as Ruth and Clark walk into the house hand in hand. I'm always so grateful that we have her, and that she has never asked intrusive questions about us or our past. I don't know how I'd cope without her.

On the way to Lemon, my mind is racing so much that I almost run a red light, and I catch myself in time but still kick myself inwardly. I cannot make stupid mistakes like that.

Around me, the sleepy town is waking up as people emerge and head for the sidewalk or their cars and bicycles. Some are holding the morning paper, a cup of coffee to go, or pressing cellphones to their ears. Several locals are already sitting outside cafés and restaurants, sipping coffee and soaking up the morning sun.

Downtown Willow Creek is a mix of old and new architecture, and the wide streets are lined with shady trees and well-tended flowerbeds.

I hold my breath when I pass the cemetery with its white picket fence and beautiful fountain in the middle of the lush garden. It always makes me think of Brett, and I wonder what his grave looks like. I've never been able to go there, to lay flowers for him and keep it as beautiful as he deserves. I'm sure his parents look after it, but I wish I could go and be with him, and talk to him even though I don't know if he can hear me.

Soon enough I arrive in the parking lot of Lemon, where the spots are separated by rows of neatly pruned bushes and shrubbery. It's shared by Lemon and a boutique fashion store.

I pull the car into an empty spot next to a black Toyota Corolla.

Before I enter Lemon, I force myself to look as though I'm not feeling well, so that Tasha doesn't think I lied to her. I don't exactly have to try hard. I know my eyes are tired-looking, with dark bags around them that still peek out from underneath my makeup.

In a weird way, today the sounds of clattering plates and people eating, laughing, chatting while they wait for their food, brings back the feeling of anxiety I used to feel in high school. Whenever I walked into the cafeteria, I felt like the popular kids were gossiping about me, even when they weren't. I was a straight-A student and a little nerdy, and that attracted a lot of attention, usually not the good kind. Now, like then, I feel as though the spotlight is on me, and everyone is seeing through me, judging, trying to figure me out.

To calm myself down, I take a deep breath, trying to fix my mind on the aromas of baked bread, fresh coffee, the faint scents rising from the jars of lemons on the tables, and the essential oil Tasha uses.

"Thank you so much for coming in, babe," Tasha says,

smiling gratefully at me. "We only need you until one p.m. Is that okay?"

"Sure." I glance at the clock. It's 10 a.m. These will be the longest three hours of my life.

I get to work immediately, but this time I'm not giving my all. I want to, and I try my best, but I don't have the strength. The little voice inside my head refuses to shut up, warning me that I'm about to be exposed. At one point, that voice is so loud I come to a standstill in the middle of the restaurant, a full tray balanced on my hand.

"Are you all right?" one of the waitresses asks me as she walks by, and I snap out of it. In a trance, I take orders and serve meals, all the while trying to avoid making eye contact with anyone.

"That's not what I ordered," a boy of about seven years old with thick hair sticking out from around his head looks up at me with disgust. "I wanted potato wedges, not French fries."

I swallow hard and glance down at my notepad. He's right, I brought him the wrong order. His mother pushes the plate in my direction, rolling her eyes, and Tasha walks by, glancing at us.

I can't afford to make mistakes. I can't put my job on the line.

"I'm so sorry." I pick up the plate of French fries.

At least I got the woman's order right, trout with a green salad.

"What do you expect me to do?" she asks. "Do you want me to start eating without my son? By the time his food gets here, I'll be done eating. And if I wait, my food will get cold."

I draw a frustrated breath and try not to feel annoyed at her exaggerated reaction. "I'll make sure it's done quickly. I'm sorry again."

I return to the kitchen.

"Hang in there, Zoe." Tasha appears from behind me. "A

few more hours and you'll be done." Her voice is understanding, but I feel terrible.

"I'm sorry." I drag a palm down one side of my face. "I'm just not feeling too well... migraine."

"Raphael keeps some Excedrin in the back. He probably wouldn't mind if you took some," she says.

"I did. It didn't help."

"I'm sorry that I had to drag you out here. But as you can see, the place is bursting at the seams."

She's right. The restaurant is loud with silverware clinking against plates on the tables, the gurgle of water glasses being filled, and the voices mixing with the sound of the music from the radio.

I give her an apologetic smile. "Don't worry. I'm fine."

Tasha squeezes my shoulder and gets back to work.

When I serve the boy his golden-brown potato wedges, he doesn't even bother to thank me, and when they are ready to leave, the woman bluntly informs me that I'll not be getting a tip.

"The food was okay, but the service needs improvement."

Tasha overhears the conversation and comes over to apologize to the woman on my behalf, but she flat-out refuses to accept the apology and grabs her son's hand. We watch them storm out of the restaurant.

"I don't know why she's making such a big fuss." Tasha's voice is on edge. "It's not as if we tried to poison her son."

I flinch and hope she didn't notice.

"I'm sorry I messed up," I say.

"Stop that." Tasha gives my arm a gentle slap. "Mistakes happen, and that wasn't even a big one."

For the rest of my shift, I make sure to do everything right. I deliver the right meals and hand back the right change.

An hour before I'm done, one of the customers gestures for me to come to the table. He's an older man with a tweed jacket and hair swept from one side of his head to the other to cover up a bald patch. "Sweetheart, would you mind turning up the volume?" He points at the TV bolted to the wall.

I nod with a smile and turn to look for the remote control. But the moment I raise my gaze to the TV, I freeze.

My face is in a corner of the screen.

Ignoring the man's request, I head to the tiny staff room and yank off my apron. My hands are trembling and I'm so dizzy, I need to get out in the fresh air before I faint.

When I'm about to leave, I almost collide with Tasha.

"I'm so sorry," I croak. "I need... I need to go now. I'm really sorry, Tasha."

Before she can respond, I head for the door.

The temperature outside is warm, but not too hot, and the sky above is clear and blue, with sunlight gleaming off the cars in the street. A hint of chocolate is in the air, from the little chocolatier next to Lemon. It's another beautiful day, but I can't slow down to take it in.

As I'm rummaging inside my bag for my car keys, I bump into someone. Without lifting my head to see who it is, I mumble an apology and push past.

"That's all right." The familiar male voice makes me turn around. It's Officer Tim Roland. He's wearing a uniform this time, and he looks even more handsome than the last time I saw him.

"You all right?" he calls out.

"Yes, thank you," I respond and speed up, sweat trickling down my spine. The last person I need to make any kind of contact with is a police officer.

Is it possible that he was in Lemon and I didn't see him? What if he saw me on TV and recognized me? As a police officer, he's trained to remember faces.

My heart is drumming hard against my chest, and my palms

are so wet I can't even get a grip on my keys. They slip from my fingers and I watch as they fall to the ground with a clink.

My nails scrape against the pavement as I grab them and run to my car. If Officer Roland didn't previously suspect I have something to hide, he probably does now. I don't look behind me, but in my panicked mind I can almost hear the sound of his footsteps, fast and steady, chasing after me.

CHAPTER 13

When I get into the car, I release the breath I didn't know I was holding and sink into the warm leather seat. I drive carefully even though I'm dying to push the car to its limit. I'm approaching a red traffic light opposite the White Cross Baptist Church when I glance in the rearview mirror and my heart stutters.

A police car is trailing me.

After the light turns green, the car flashes its lights and I pull over, feeling sick to my stomach.

I listen to the thud of boots on the pavement, counting each step until the officer reaches my car.

Maybe it's nothing. I could have a broken taillight I didn't notice.

Stop kidding yourself, the little voice scoffs.

I take several deep breaths, forcing myself to stay calm.

When he reaches my car, he plants a gloved hand on the roof. It is, indeed, Officer Roland.

Sweat is pouring from every pore of my body.

"Are you okay, Zoe? Looks like you need this." He reaches into his pocket and hands me a bone-white handkerchief.

"Thanks." The word comes out in a whisper.

I keep my eyes averted as I dab at my face, hoping I'm not removing the heavy makeup I wear nowadays. The handkerchief smells of his cologne, a woodsy, masculine scent. As I hand it back to him, he curls his fingers over mine. His hand is warm, and his touch sends ripples of heat up my arm.

"Please keep it. I don't use handkerchiefs. I keep an entire box of them in my trunk and I hand them out to people in distress." He winks and gives me a smile that makes me a little breathless. "My father raised me to be a true gentleman."

Suppressing a shiver, I ease my hand out of his grip. "Thanks," I say again and wish I could vanish into the ground.

"Are you sure you're okay?" he asks again, genuine concern in his voice.

"Did I do something wrong, Officer?" I ask and instantly wonder if that was the wrong thing to say. "I mean... yes, I'm fine." My lips tremble into a fake smile as I stuff the handkerchief into my handbag.

"Good to hear." He folds his arms over his chest. "Now, why would you think you've done something wrong?"

When I don't respond because I can't find the right words, he clears his throat and continues. "You looked unwell when you were leaving the restaurant, and I was worried about you on the road. I thought you might need some help."

"Umm... thank you, but you don't need to be concerned. I'm fine."

He scrutinizes me with his piercing eyes. "Why don't I believe you? You really don't look well."

That's because I'm on the verge of fainting, I want to say, but I keep the words inside my head.

"You're right. I'm not feeling too good today, I have a terrible migraine."

"Then it might not be a good idea for you to drive. I'd be happy to drive you."

"No, don't worry about it," I say quickly. "I'm well enough to drive."

"How far from here do you live?"

Wrong question. I don't want him to know where I live.

"Not far." I let out a nervous giggle. "I'll be home soon."

"Good, I'll drive behind you, then. I just want to make sure you arrive safely."

"Please don't trouble yourself. I'm sure you have more important work to do."

"I'm on a break. I was looking forward to a cup of coffee at Lemon, but I prefer to help folks out when I can."

I clutch my hands in my lap, unsure what more to tell him.

"That's very kind. Thank you." I have no choice but to accept the offer, but I'm almost hyperventilating as I watch him walking back to his car.

This is bad, a train wreck waiting to happen, but I can't stop it.

He drives behind me as he promised he would.

My plan was to go to Ruth's to pick up Clark, but I don't want Officer Roland to know that I have a son. Afraid to arrive at my cabin, I drive slowly. But before long, we're turning into the dirt road that leads up to it. I'm hyper aware of everything: the tall trees on either side of my car, the dusty sand beneath its wheels, the warm air coming in through the window and the sweat that makes my clothes stick to my skin.

I pull up in front of the cabin and get out of my car, and the police officer does the same.

He gazes at the cabin. "This is where you live?" he asks in a tone that gives nothing away.

"Yep. That's my home."

"Looks like it needs some work done on it. I'm quite handy if you ever need a little help with any repairs."

Among other things, the paint is peeling, and a portion of

the wall is water stained. I think it's a pretty cabin, but he's right that it needs a lot of work.

"That's a kind offer, but I'm okay, thanks. Looks can be deceiving; the inside isn't so bad."

In another life, I'd invite him in so I could make him the coffee he missed at his lunch break, but right now that would be asking for trouble. He won't get to see the chipped bathroom tiles, the discolored walls, and the missing baseboards. I've done a lot in the past months to make the cabin more comfortable for us, but what really matters is that it's private and the price is right. For that I'm grateful.

My phone is ringing inside my bag. It must be Tasha wanting to know what's going on with me. Guilt stabs me when I think of what I did to her, leaving her hanging when she needed me. How would she feel if she found out that I'd been lying to her for months about who I really am?

Officer Roland attempts to make small talk, but he soon figures out that I'm not in the mood to chat, so he gets back into his car. Before he drives off, I come to my senses and call after him, thanking him for his help.

"No problem," he says through the window. "It's my job." He grins. "Will I see you at Lemon tomorrow?"

"I... I'm going to be off for a few days, but I'll see you around." I give him a wave as he drives away.

I pray to God he's not interested in me. Even if Tasha wants me to date, and I'd be lying if I said I don't find him attractive, being involved with a cop would obviously be a big mistake.

Safely inside the cabin, I return Tasha's call and apologize.

"Zoe, I'm really concerned about you."

"Don't be, I'm okay. I'm truly sorry."

"I get that you're not feeling well, but you really shouldn't just run out like that."

I press a hand to my forehead. The headache I lied about having is slowly becoming real. "I couldn't stay. I'm sorry."

"Is there anything you want to talk to me about?"

"No." The word comes flooding out. "There's nothing. I'm fine. I'll be fine."

"You can trust me, Zoe. I hope you know that."

She has a good heart, but I can't trust anyone at this point. I'm desperate to lean on someone, but what I want and what I need to do are in conflict.

I cannot let my mask slip under any circumstances.

After a short silence, she speaks again. "Maybe it's none of my business, but when you said you had a migraine, it didn't seem like you were telling the whole truth. Seems like you've got something more going on, something emotional."

I have to give her something, something she can hold onto so she doesn't continue digging.

"Being a single mother is tough sometimes," I say.

"I know it must be." She pauses. "You know what, go ahead and take a few days off. We'll manage."

I swallow the tears lingering in my throat. "Thank you."

When we hang up, I run to the kitchen and pour myself a glass of water. My throat is parched. I should go and pick up Clark, but I don't want him to see me in this state. I need to be alone, to think.

I sit in front of the TV and flip through the channels. Sooner or later, Brett's murder will be reported again. Sure enough, soon it's up on one of the local news channels. According to the reporters, the police department in Fort Haven has been getting calls from people who claim to have seen me. They don't elaborate, so I can't tell if the callers are from Willow Creek or another town. There are so many people who would lie for a reward of $20,000.

Breathe, just breathe.

Switching off the TV, I run myself a cool bath and hope it will calm me down. The cabin bathroom is cozy with natural wood walls, distressed cabinets, and vintage-looking faucets and fixtures. But like everything else, it needs some work. While I wait for the free-standing tub to fill up, I wet a cloth in the sink and run it over the soapstone countertops to remove the dust that constantly accumulates there no matter how hard I try to keep them clean.

Once my bath is ready, I sink into the water, cringing at the cold before submerging my head and face.

What if I just eliminated myself before the cops find me?

But how could I do that to Clark?

When my lungs start to scream for oxygen, I emerge from the water, splashing it everywhere, gasping for air. As soon as my breathing finally gets back to normal, I get out of the tub, almost slipping on the wooden tiles.

As I wrap myself in my bathrobe and head to the bedroom to get dressed, I am suddenly overcome with the feeling of being watched. Turning to the open window and looking out into the trees, I feel my skin crawl. There is no one in sight, just the tree branches moving in the gentle breeze and the tree shadows stirring, but my gut tells me someone is there. I get dressed fast, the hairs on the back of my neck standing at attention.

Before I leave the room, I look back out of the window and stare hard into the trees, but there's no one. That powerful feeling of unease persists, a fog wrapping its tendrils around me. I feel deeply unsafe, and terribly alone.

CHAPTER 14

Instead of running from my past, it's time I face it head-on. I grab one of the notepads lying around the cabin and a pen. Then I sink onto the couch and write down everything that pops into my head about the night that my life changed forever. As I make notes, writing down every detail I remember, from the time I took the syringe up to Brett to when I found him dead, I can't stop thinking about the conversation I had with Laurel, the look in her eye when she dared me to keep her away from my husband.

I jot down on paper that I saw her smoking a cigarette outside when I returned from my run. I can see why she would want to end Brett's suffering, as she was so close to him. But did she hate me to the point that she would want me to go down for murder?

When my head is empty of memories from that night, I switch on the TV and flip through the channels, but there are no more reports on the murder. I need more information to help me put the puzzle together. It's impossible without the internet, but I can't go back to Lemon right now. There is a library a few blocks from where Ruth lives, with computers that people can use.

I'll stop by before I buy groceries to last us a few days and pick up Clark.

Before I leave the cabin, I double-check that all the doors and windows are closed. Again, as I walk toward my car, I feel that creeping sensation down my spine, and I tell myself it's just my nerves. Nobody is there. I'm all alone.

*

The library is a small one-story red-brick building with stained glass windows, a cheery sunflower garden at the front and a small wooden bench by the entrance, where a chessboard sits in the center and two gray-haired men are facing off.

Inside, the walls are lined with shelves holding thousands of books. The air is musty and smells of old paper and floor polish. Aside from two women reading on one of the couches, there's hardly anyone around.

I walk to the computer area and head straight to a table in the back corner, settling into a worn green chair, and I turn the computer on and wait for it to boot up. Then I pull out my notebook and pen. At first, I read all the articles about Brett's death again, noting any information that stands out. Then I start watching videos of news snippets.

After searching for Laurel's name, I'm shocked to stumble upon a video of a Fort Haven reporter interviewing her about Brett's death and their friendship. She's all dolled up for the interview in a red tank top and black skin-tight jeans, her blonde hair hanging loosely around her shoulders, her dark eyes clear and steady as she gazes into the camera.

Something is different about her, but I can't figure out what it is.

She and the reporter are sitting in front of her and Marjorie's house. Their porch looks camera-ready with candles—even in the daylight—and a large arrangement of peach roses, carnations, and lilies. Even the wall of the house looks like it has a fresh coat of pale-pink paint. I'm so glad that the house I shared with Brett is not shown on camera. I don't know if I could bear to see it.

The reporter, a middle-aged woman with a round full face and short dark hair, asks, "How do you feel, now that it's been a year and Brett Wilton's murderer still hasn't been brought to justice?"

Laurel sighs. "It was so painful finding out that my best friend died, but to know that he was murdered broke my heart. And his poor parents still haven't recovered from the loss of their son and grandson." She pauses to wipe her eyes even though I can't see any tears. "It's been hard for his mother especially. I pray every day that his murderer will be brought to justice, so the people who loved Brett can have some closure."

"Are you close with the Wilton family?" the reporter asks.

"Yes, especially now as we grieve Brett. I have known him since we were in school and I was almost like the Wiltons' second child because I spent so much time in their home. Our mothers are really close as well."

"Was there anything romantic between you and Brett, when you were growing up?" the reporter asks with a tilt of her head.

Laurel shakes her head but hesitates for just a few seconds before answering. "No, never. I would say we were just very good friends."

"And you never felt anything more than friendship for him?"

Laurel blushes beneath her makeup and lifts a glass of water to her lips. "That's a rather personal question, don't you think?" she asks innocently, but her tone says it all.

I remove my glasses and pinch the bridge of my nose. I wish

the reporter would ask more questions about Brett's death, so I can see how she reacts.

"I apologize, Miss Smith. I was just curious." The reporter crosses her legs. "Tell me about Brett. What kind of man was he?"

"The best. He was a kind and gentle soul. I miss him terribly. I keep thinking about the last time I saw him, lying sick in his bed. It was awful seeing him like that."

"And he was very generous, according to most people in town. Is it true that he left you his Cadillac Escalade?"

Laurel nods, then blushes again as if she had not meant to reveal that information.

I'm staring at the screen in shock. Brett left her his favorite car? He could have left it for Clark for when he grew up.

"He must have cared for you very much." The reporter pauses. "Miss Smith, in your opinion, do you think it's possible that Brett's wife killed her own husband?"

"There's no doubt in my mind that she did. She married Brett for his money, everyone knows that. She used to work as a maid at the Wiltons' hotel. Brett was already very ill when he died, but I think she just couldn't wait to get her hands on his money, and she was tired of caring for him. I wouldn't even be surprised if she made his illness worse, it all happened way too quickly. She killed him, and she deserves to go to prison for the rest of her life."

Anger raging through me, I close the video and write down what I know.

Brett left Laurel his Cadillac.

After catching my breath, I click the video again and brace myself, but for the rest of the time, she only goes on about how she believes I murdered Brett. When the video comes to an end, I sit in silence with my eyes closed and my head pounding.

I can't give up. I need to keep digging. If Laurel did something to Brett, I need to find out. And the one person who knows her better than anyone is her mother.

I open my eyes again and type in the Fort Haven town website address.

The site boasts the local attractions, yearly events, and even a phone directory that enables locals to stay in touch. I click on the phone directory page and scroll to the letter S. I don't know yet what I want to ask Marjorie, but I'll think of something.

When I recall how comfortable Laurel was in front of the camera, an idea hits me. If there's anyone who loves attention more than she does, it's her mother, and at the end of Laurel's interview, she mentioned that she and her mother were open to more interviews, to continue speaking about Brett so his name is never forgotten and to remind people to keep an eye out for me.

Instead of calling Marjorie on my phone, I drive to the nearest payphone. I got rid of my old cell when we went on the run, and I use a prepaid phone now. It's hard for burners to be traced, but it's not impossible. I don't want to take chances.

Ignoring the stench of urine in the little cubicle, I slide a coin into the machine.

As soon as the phone starts ringing, it's picked up. "Marjorie Smith at your service. How can I help?" She has clearly rehearsed this, hoping that the press will contact her.

"Hello," I say, holding my nose to disguise the real sound of my voice. "My name is Linda Simone from the Fort Haven Tribune. I was informed that you are willing to answer questions pertaining to the murder of Mr. Brett Wilton."

"That's right," Marjorie chirps. "I will do anything that assists in the capture of the woman who murdered him."

I'm silent for a moment, and as I taste metal, I realize I've bitten down hard on my lip. "Thank you, ma'am. I don't want to waste your time, so let's jump right in."

"Perfect," she says. "Would you mind it very much if at the

end of the interview you give me an email address? I'd like to send you the photo I want you to use of myself."

"Sure, no problem. Now, will you please explain to me exactly what happened that day?"

She clears her throat. "Well, as I told the police and other reporters, I was having a hard time sleeping that night, and when that happens, I read a book. I was in the middle of a chapter when I saw lights flashing outside and I looked out to see an ambulance. I knew right away that something terrible must have happened to Brett Wilton, who was very ill. Later, when I spoke to Nora Wilton, who is a good friend of mine, I found out that her son had died." She pauses for breath. "When my daughter Laurel and I heard he had been killed, we knew immediately that his wife had done it."

"What do you believe the reason was?" I ask, tightening my fingers around the phone. "Why would she kill her husband?"

"For the money, of course. And because it's hard, caring for someone when they are so unwell, particularly if you never really loved them. Also, only a guilty person would run."

I draw in a deep breath. No more beating around the bush, I need to say something she will not expect. One thing I do know about Marjorie is that her husband died three years ago, leaving her and her daughter in deep debt, and there were rumors that they were selling the house last year. But they are still in that house, and on the video, it looked like it had been given an impressive makeover.

"Miss Smith, do you truly believe that Meghan Wilton killed her husband, or did you receive compensation in exchange for telling the public that she did? You and your daughter have been very vocal about it. Do you care to comment on that?"

First there's silence, then the phone goes dead.

It's fine. She answered my question without saying a word.

CHAPTER 15

Taking matters into my own hands gives me a burst of energy I haven't felt in a while. When I arrive at Ruth's house to pick up Clark, the anxiety that loomed over me earlier has dimmed.

I'm sure now that I didn't kill Brett in my sleep. But I'm still terrified of the police catching up with me before I have concrete evidence to prove that someone else did it. But since leaving the library, my thoughts have been churning around about Laurel, and also about Jane. I didn't know what motive she would have for killing Brett, but I can't ignore the fact that she was in the house as well. And she said she saw me take the syringe upstairs, but I'm certain there was nobody around when I did. She lied.

Could she have found the full syringe and decided to put him out of his misery? Was that why she acted so strange when I told her about his death? Is this why she's pinning the blame on me?

Ruth is not out on the porch with Clark like she normally is, and I get out of the car and hurry up the porch steps to the red door, listening to the wood creak under my feet.

It takes a while for her to come to the door, and while I wait, I look behind me at the houses on the other side of the road.

In the house opposite Ruth's, a little girl is playing with a large dollhouse in the yard, while her mother arranges the flowerbeds in the front. The mother is tall and thin, with short blonde hair, and she is wearing a white dress that looks too fancy for gardening. Next to their house, a woman hangs out the laundry on the line. Everyone here seems to have such picture-perfect lives.

I ring the bell again and take out my phone, checking the time. Finally, Ruth comes to the door, all smiles.

"Sorry, darling, I didn't hear the bell. We were out in the back, planting marigolds."

"I have my own flowerbed, Mommy." Clark emerges from behind Ruth.

"Is that so?" I throw her a quick smile. "That sounds like fun."

"So much fun! Mrs. Foster said she's going to get more seeds for us tomorrow."

"But we're celebrating your birthday tomorrow, Superboy. We'll be spending the day together, remember?"

Clark's birthday was three months ago, but I was going through a severe bout of depression at the time and was unable to give him the attention he deserved. It was his idea to move his birthday to another date this year.

His face crumples, but only for a second before he perks up again. It would have crushed me if he would rather spend time with Ruth than with me. I wouldn't have blamed him, though. I've not been the mother he deserves lately.

"Why don't you do something different today?" Ruth rests a hand on top of Clark's head.

"What do you mean?" I tilt my head to the side.

"Instead of rushing back to the cabin, I was thinking maybe

the two of you could have an early dinner with me. It's been a while."

"I'm not sure." I shift from one foot to the other. Although I appreciate her invitation, I was looking forward to being alone with Clark. "We kind of have plans."

"Plans can be changed, can't they? I would certainly appreciate the company." Her eyes are pleading.

Ruth is such a lovely person, and my heart really goes out to her. She lost her husband eleven years ago, and she has no children to keep her company. I think of insisting that we have to go, but the sadness in her eyes makes me change my mind. How could I refuse her an hour or two of my time?

"Okay, sure. That sounds wonderful." I step into the house that always smells of fresh laundry and vanilla candles. "I hope you haven't gone to too much trouble."

"Not yet." She laughs. "Silly me, the idea to invite you to dinner just came to me now. I haven't even given thought about what I will feed you. I'll come up with something."

It's already close to 6 p.m., which is when Clark usually eats, and when Ruth cooks, she takes forever. We've been to her place for dinner before and we ended up staying for over three hours, and I'm just a little too tired for that right now. So, as I'm closing the door, I suggest that I cook something while she relaxes with Clark. I know my way around her kitchen already, so it won't be hard to find a few random ingredients and rustle up a quick meal.

She lays a hand on her chest. "I can't let you do that. *You* need to rest. You've been working all day. It must have been busy at the restaurant for Tasha to let you work longer than you'd planned."

Of course, she doesn't know that I left work early.

"That's all right." I wave a dismissive hand, ignoring my guilt. "I have plenty of energy left."

"Can you make lasagna?" Clark asks and I laugh.

"It depends on what Mrs. Foster has in the kitchen." I glance at her again, questioningly. "And if I'm allowed to cook."

Ruth gives my arm a pat. "If it's really no bother, I would appreciate it. You're such a great cook."

While Clark and Ruth are back in the garden tending to their flowerbeds, I rummage around in the kitchen in search of ingredients. Ruth's kitchen also has a fairy-tale feel. The cabinet doors are painted in pastel shades, and they're pristine, free of fingerprints or dust. I open the pale-pink fridge, and the cool air escapes, making my skin prickle. There are fresh fruits and vegetables on the counter, but aside from chicken wings thawing in a Ziploc plastic bag on the low shelf, the contents of the fridge are limited to mainly the basics – water, juice, milk, butter, and yogurt. I close the fridge and walk into the pantry at the other end of the kitchen. In contrast to the refrigerator, it's fully stocked.

All kinds of food supplies are stacked on the shelves; everything clearly marked with black and white stickers. Flour, rice, sugar, pasta, and bottle after bottle of condiments are categorized by type and expiration date. I can't even imagine how many hours Ruth must have spent sorting and organizing everything.

I run a finger along the metal edge of the top shelf that's lined with baking ingredients, and smile as I suddenly imagine myself standing inside a bakery that I own.

I don't find lasagna sheets, so I decide to cook fried rice with vegetables and chicken. While I cook, I try to clear my mind and make myself a promise that when I'm with my son, I'll do my best to be present. It's going to be hard, but I'll give it my all.

As I savor the scent of the chicken frying and hum gently to myself, I find the act of cooking so therapeutic that I even make a dessert. When Ruth and Clark return to the kitchen in time for the food, they're both smiling from ear to ear.

"It all smells wonderful." Ruth beams. "One day, when you open up that restaurant or bakery, I'll be your first customer."

I smile and distract myself with serving the food. Thinking about the future is a luxury I can't afford right now. It's safer to only focus on surviving the present.

"Clark, is this better than lasagna?" I ask.

He nods and shoves a spoonful of fried rice into his mouth, his eyes gleaming.

Ruth and I smile at each other. Right now, in her cozy kitchen, I feel normal. I feel free even though I know that, at any moment, my joy could be stolen again and replaced with pain and fear.

I like to pretend we're a family: me, Clark, and Ruth. The gentle way she talks to him and touches him when she stands to get some water, her hand resting on his shoulder before brushing his hair off his forehead. It all makes it easy for me to fool myself.

I'm about to serve the fruit and cream I whipped up for dessert when the doorbell rings, and Ruth frowns.

"That's odd. I'm not expecting visitors." She wipes her mouth and pushes back her chair. "I'll be right back, dears."

I glance at the kitchen clock. It's close to eight; the time has gone by so fast. I hope that Ruth won't invite the person in; I want to remain in our safe bubble a little longer. Straining my ears, I try to hear her speaking to the person at the door. There's a male voice, and he sounds upset. But I'm unable to catch the words because he's speaking at a high speed and Ruth is lowering her voice.

I jolt at the sound of the door slamming. Everything is silent until, suddenly, someone appears at the kitchen window. Clark drops his spoon. Looking in at us is the face of a strange, angry man with long, greasy hair and tattoos on one side of his neck.

"Mommy, I'm scared." Clark runs over to me and hides his face in my chest.

"It's all right, baby," I say, staring nervously back at the man, who squints at us for a few seconds before walking away.

Who is he, and what did he want from Ruth?

When she comes back into the kitchen, she's not the same woman who had left. The sparkle in her eyes has disappeared. I want to tell her about the man at the window, but she's upset enough.

"Who was it?" I ask, desperate to know.

"Nobody." She wipes her hands on a kitchen towel as if she had washed them. "No one at all."

When she turns around again, her eyes are wet. "I hope you don't mind, but I'm rather tired already." She forces a laugh. "Old age is certainly catching up with me. Please feel free to stay and enjoy your dessert. I apologize for being such a terrible host."

With that, she kisses Clark on the top of the head and squeezes my shoulder. Then she shuffles out of the kitchen. With her shoulders hunched even more, she looks much shorter.

It feels uncomfortable to be eating dessert without her around, so I tell Clark we should leave. He doesn't want to, but I don't give him a choice. I do my best to explain to him that Mrs. Foster is not feeling well, and she needs to rest.

Back at the cabin when I close my eyes to sleep, the man from the window revisits me, his eyes narrowed as though he's trying to read my thoughts. Who is he and why did Ruth seem so upset by his visit? Most importantly, is he a danger to me and my son?

CHAPTER 16

I wake up shortly before midnight. Frustrated, I slide out of the covers, careful not to wake Clark, and sit on the edge of the bed. His gentle breathing is interrupted by an occasional snore. I want to get back into bed, put my arms around him, and make him a silent promise that everything will be all right. But I'm cautious about making promises I might not be able to keep.

As I rise to my feet, it suddenly occurs to me that something woke me up, and it wasn't a nightmare. It must have been a noise from the forest outside, perhaps a fox or another wild animal. I tiptoe out of the room and close the door behind me, heading to the kitchen.

It's late, but the only thing that will calm me down is baking. I planned on waking up early anyway to make Clark's cake, and since I'm already up, I might as well do it now. I gather all the ingredients I need and jump right in.

A sharp cracking sound catches my attention. It's coming from outside.

The blinds are closed and I'm afraid to peek. Standing still at the stove, my ears strain to listen to more sounds, and every muscle in my body is on high alert.

When I don't hear anything else, I exhale and get back to my baking, burying my hands into the silky flour. I'm just on edge. It's not the first time I've imagined something that's not there.

Within minutes, the mixture is ready, and the heady aromas of vanilla and chocolate make me smile. Maybe I should have waited to bake the cake with Clark, to create another memory together, but he also loves surprises. I'm taking him out, too, for a special treat. It's a risk, but he begged me to take him to the park, and it felt awful to hear my son beg to be outdoors.

A memory from the past comes to me. On Clark's third birthday, Brett and I took him to Disneyland. To my horror, I discovered that Nora was also there, staying at the same hotel. I had asked Brett not to share our plans with his mom.

It was a chance to be just the three of us, and I wanted to enjoy my family without her constant shadow. But somehow, she knew. Jane had told her, she said, and she wanted to surprise us. She didn't get the reaction she expected from me, and the whole weekend was ruined. Nora ended up stealing the show, buying gifts for Clark that cost a fortune, like a toy train that Clark loved so much he took it almost everywhere with him. It's the only toy he brought with him from Fort Haven.

I'll do whatever I can to make this birthday special. I'll give him another missing piece of his childhood, a happy memory to hold onto in an uncertain future.

While the cake is baking, I sit at the kitchen table with the notes I made about the night my husband died. My eyes scan the page, where I scribbled down notes from Laurel's interview and my conversation with Marjorie. Then, with a heavy heart, I add Jane's name to the list and I decide that I need to find out where she is now.

Since I'll be taking Clark out of town to go to a park, I'll find a payphone somewhere and make a call to the Fort Haven Black

Oyster Hotel. Since Jane quit working at our house, I figure she may have returned to working at the hotel.

Another sound makes me jump, and I straighten up so fast my back cracks. It's also coming from outside the house. Is it a tree branch breaking, or is it something else?

I inch over to the window just as the blinds start to glow, as though someone is pointing a bright light toward the cabin.

Someone is out there.

Have Brett's parents found me?

I run to the switch, flick off the light, and press my back against the wall. The room remains illuminated by the light outside for a few seconds before the light goes out again. Then, just as my eyes are adjusting to the darkness, whoever is outside turns the light back on.

My mouth grows drier with each second.

A moment passes before panic brings my body to life, and I run through the cabin, checking that all the windows are closed and the curtains or blinds are shut. Then I look in the bedroom to make sure Clark is okay. He's still fast asleep. I might have to wake him so we can escape into the woods. I've thought about this before, always praying it would never happen.

I return to the kitchen and force myself to move to the window. Whoever is out there is taunting me again, switching the light on and off.

Then the light stays on.

Unmistakably, a car door slams and my stomach clenches.

I hold my breath as I open the blinds a few inches. A figure is standing in front of a pickup truck. The blinding headlights make it hard for me to see the person's face.

The silence around me is so thick and I can't see any movement in the tree branches outside. It's as if the forest has stopped breathing. Like me, the trees look like they're waiting to see what's going to happen next.

The figure starts walking toward the kitchen window and

my mind tells me to let go of the blinds, but I can't get myself to; my hand feels paralyzed. He emerges from the harsh yellow light and comes closer to the cabin, and my breath catches in my throat. It's the man with the tattoos, the one who came to Ruth's home. He gives me a slow smile, looking straight at me. He must be able to see me peering through the blinds. Then he turns to walk back to his truck. He slides behind the wheel and starts the engine, and finally he drives off.

Weak with fear, I crumple to the floor, my hands covering my mouth. Who is he? And what does he want? It's exhausting to think I will have to worry about someone else now on top of the police, Nora, and Cole. Whoever it is, he scares the hell out of me.

I make sure once more that the doors and windows are locked, even though I know they are. Then I open the kitchen blinds and gaze down the path where his truck disappeared. My eyes are still blurry from the bright lights, and my heart feels like it's cowering in a corner of my body, afraid to come out. Not even baking can help with how I'm feeling right now. I switch off the oven: the cake will be ruined, but I can't finish. The magic is gone.

The only thing I want to do is hold my son.

My heart still pounding, I slide into bed and tighten an arm around his warm little body. I'm holding him, but he's the one that's holding me together.

CHAPTER 17

A week after the stranger showed up at the cabin, I'm back at work for the first time. He left me on edge and unable to sleep much at night, always waiting for the sound of tires on the path outside. The worst of it was the fact that I was so tormented that Clark's birthday didn't go as planned. I managed to finish the football chocolate cake. I sang to him and we danced around, but I wasn't there at all mentally, and I know he felt it. Everything was ruined again. I couldn't fake being happy and excited, and I found it hard to focus on him when my emotions were in turmoil. Clark asked me several times if I was all right, and I felt consumed with guilt. I had failed him yet again.

I've been waiting every day for the man to return, but he never did.

Until now.

He's standing in the doorway of Lemon. The same greasy hair brushes his shoulders, and a sneer stretches across his lips as our eyes meet. I'm tempted to run, but I can't let Tasha down again.

"Great," Tasha says next to me. "Just what we need today."

Her eyes are on the stranger, who is now making his way

toward one of the tables in the back. Once seated, he reaches into his back pocket for a pack of cigarettes, and he pulls one from the pack and lights it.

"Hell no." Tasha hurries over to the table. I can't hear what she's telling him, but her expression says it all. To my horror, while keeping his eyes on her face he turns the cigarette upside down and presses the glowing tip into the table. Smoke curls upward and it burns through the tablecloth.

"Get out of here now," Tasha nearly shouts, and she yanks the tablecloth off. The man stands and looks past her in my direction before he leaves, still smirking horribly.

Why is he so interested in me?

"If he weren't Ruth's son, I swear I would have called the cops on him." Tasha's chest is rising and falling rapidly as she makes her way back to me. "It's hard to believe that someone like that could come from such a gentle and kind woman." She hugs the folded tablecloth to her body.

"Ruth has a son?" The revelation sends a ripple of surprise through me. I don't understand; she told me that she doesn't have kids.

Tasha hands the tablecloth to one of the other waitresses. "Yes, his name is Luke. I'm surprised you didn't know that." She frowns at me. "I just assumed you did since you and Ruth are pretty close."

"I *did* see him before... once. But I don't know him."

"Well, it's in your best interest to keep as far away from him as you can." At the sound of someone coming through the door, she turns away from me. "Let's catch up in a bit. My favorite guests have arrived."

It's Martha and Julius, a couple in their nineties who come to Lemon every single Monday at the same time. They always order the same meal: a potato and tuna casserole, which they eat while holding hands. It's very sweet and I can't help wondering if me and Brett would have been like that, if he'd lived to see old age.

The thought of him being gone makes me feel hollow, but I bite my lip to keep from crying, and I push the pain away until later, focusing on the here and now instead of what could have been.

Tasha leaves me standing by the bar, trying to process what I heard, and I finally pull myself together and serve a group of teenagers.

"One grilled cheese sandwich, one hamburger with fries." I'm trying to focus, but my mind keeps spiraling back to Luke, and his inexplicable obsession with me. Why would he care about me at all?

I find Tasha in the kitchen soon afterwards. "I didn't even know Ruth had kids," I say.

"Well, you saw him. I wouldn't be surprised if she wants to pretend Luke doesn't exist. Word around town is that he killed his twin brother."

"Oh my God. That's... That's so scary." My mind goes back to the night he parked in front of the cabin while my son slept peacefully. "Why isn't he in prison?"

"He was never found guilty. The story goes that, a few years ago, Luke went boating with his brother, Daniel, and only he returned. But apparently, the police had never been able to find enough evidence to nail him. He *did* just come out of prison for something else, though. Drug-related, I think." Tasha pours iced tea into several glasses and places them on the silver tray. She balances it on her flat palm. "I feel sorry for Ruth. He really made her life hell. People are kind of hoping he'll commit another crime just so he'll go back to prison and leave her alone."

Tasha walks away, leaving me shaken. I'm relieved that this dangerous man has nothing to do with my past, but I just don't understand why he's so interested in me, and I'm concerned that he might end up blowing my cover. He's clearly onto some-thing: but how much does he know? Or how much will he find out?

The rest of the day passes in a blur, and when I go to pick up Clark, I find Luke's truck parked in front of the house across from Ruth's. He's sitting inside, smoke from a cigarette curling in wisps out the window, and his gaze is focused on the house.

Even though I've spent so many months trying to avoid them, if he shows up at the cabin again, I might call the cops. He could be a danger to Ruth. Or even to my son. For the first time, I wish that I had made friends with Officer Roland.

I try not to look at Luke's truck as I make my way down the path to Ruth's door. But his gaze is burning holes in my back. While I wait for Ruth to open the door, I glance over my shoulder briefly and he gives me a curt nod. I turn away, my hands sweating as I ring the bell again. When she opens the door, Ruth hands Clark over to me and quickly closes it again without acknowledging her son. I barely get a chance to say anything to her, she's far from her usual chatty self.

When I get into my car, I glimpse her peering out through the living room window.

I can't imagine feeling afraid of my own son.

You have your own problems. The voice inside my head is urging me to drive away, to leave her behind. She clearly didn't want to talk to me about it, and she's been managing with this relationship for years. She will be okay, and I need to get my son away.

I drive fast, but I don't head toward the cabin. The best place to be if Luke is after us for some reason is among other people rather than in an isolated cabin in the woods.

"Where are we going, Mommy?" Clark asks when I don't turn down the dirt road that leads into the woods.

"I thought maybe we could drive around town for a bit before it gets dark."

He doesn't object; he appreciates anything that keeps him out of the house. I allow him to choose the music on the radio, and I pretend to be having as much fun as he is, but my hands are trembling on the wheel.

I wish I knew why Luke drove all the way to my cabin that night. He knew he was scaring me. But what have I ever done to him?

CHAPTER 18

Clark and I are hiding out in our cabin. I haven't taken him to Ruth's for two days now, which also means I didn't get to go to work. Money is tight, but I'm too afraid of Luke and the danger he could present to my son. I need to keep Clark away, until I know more or until Luke has disappeared again.

"I don't understand," Ruth said over the phone when I told her I wasn't dropping Clark off at her house. "I don't mind taking care of your little boy. Surely you know that."

"Yes," I said. "I do, and I appreciate it so much but—"

"Then what's the problem?"

I squeezed my eyes shut. "Nothing. I just want to spend more time with Clark. I've been working so much."

I wanted to tell Ruth the truth, but Luke is her son. It must be painful enough for her without me turning the knife too. Part of me wonders if they might even rebuild the relationship, but if they do, I'm not sure I can continue to leave Clark in her care. He will be devastated not to see her anymore, but it's not worth the risk. I'll have to find a way to manage without her.

It's possible that I could take Clark with me to work: Tasha wouldn't mind, but after the other day I'm even worried that

Luke could turn up there. I don't want him anywhere near my son.

"Mommy, do you want to play Memory with me?"

"Yes, absolutely." I glance up at Clark from the book I've been failing to read, too absorbed in my own thoughts. "But first, I want us to go into town for a bit."

"Can we go to Mrs. Foster's today?"

"No, baby. I just need to make a call."

"But you have a phone. There it is." He points at my cell phone on the couch next to me.

"It's not... I don't have enough credit."

"Can we go to the park after you're finished?"

"I'm sorry, sweetie. Can I take a raincheck?"

I feel terrible for breaking so many promises to him. He deserves so much more than this; he deserves a happy, playful childhood. He should have friends his own age. He should have his father back. I'm just so afraid, and it's constricting everything he does. The more I put us out there, the more chances we give someone to figure out who we are. It's too risky.

"But I gave you so many rainchecks already." He plants his hands on his hips, his eyes flashing with anger.

"You're right." I gesture for him to come closer. "I'm so sorry."

He lays his head on my lap and I stroke his hair, enjoying the warmth of his scalp. He loves it when I soothe him that way.

"This is the last raincheck," he murmurs. "Can we go next Saturday? And when I finish playing, can we eat a burger at a restaurant?"

"Okay," I say.

He sits up suddenly, his eyes gleaming with excitement. "You promise?"

It doesn't matter how many promises I have broken; he still believes in me. He's still prepared to give me another chance.

"I promise." I kiss his forehead.

I have to keep this one. I'll just have to take the chance, and hope that everything will be okay.

As we leave the cabin, as always, I scan the surroundings nervously. The mountains loom in the distance and the trees sway lazily in the breeze, casting twisted shadows on the forest floor. Except for the rustle of leaves and the chirp of birds in the branches, everything is silent. I should be reassured, but I don't fully trust the peaceful scene. It's hard for me to trust anything right now.

I keep waiting for Luke to show up at the door, but he hasn't been back since that night with the headlights. Maybe he's leaving me alone. But what message was he trying to send me? Why did he want me to be afraid? Is he jealous of the relationship I have with Ruth? Does he want us out of the cabin so he can have it?

I buckle Clark into his car seat and slide behind the wheel. In my head, I'm already rehearsing the conversation I'll have with whoever answers the phone in the Black Oyster housekeeping department. I know it's risky to call there, but I'm going to try to disguise my voice, so nobody recognizes me and notifies Cole and Nora, or the police. I'm taking things one step at a time, and I'm not sure what I'll do next if I do find out that Jane is still there.

But nobody else is anywhere near the truth of what happened to Brett. I'm the only person who can clear my name.

I don't go to the same payphone I used to call Marjorie, driving instead to one on the edge of town. By the time we arrive, Clark is asleep. I drive as close as I can get to a phone box with skulls painted on the side and leave him sleeping peacefully while I make the call. Aside from a dry cleaner and a gas station, there's not much around.

The floor of the phone box is littered with dirty and torn

newspapers on the floor and someone has scrawled "talk is cheap" in blue marker across the glass door. The interior is hot and stuffy and smells just as awful as the last one. I try not to breathe through my nose as I pick up the grimy cream receiver and drop my coins in the slot, waiting for the tone to sound. My hand is sweaty as I dial the number, and I lean against the side of the booth, watching the traffic go by as the phone begins to ring.

"Housekeeping. How may I help you?" I don't recognize the voice of the woman who answers in a low and flat monotone. She probably never knew me, but I still need to be cautious.

I lower my voice and hope it sounds different enough. "Hi, my name is Rosemary Fox. I'm trying to get in touch with one of your employees, her name is Jane Drew. Does she still work at your hotel?"

"I'm afraid she's no longer working here," she says a little too quickly.

"Oh, okay," I say. "Would you happen to know where she is, by any chance?"

Silence.

"Hello? Are you still there?"

"I'm here." I detect a note of unease in the woman's voice. "What is this about exactly?"

I run a hand through my hair, trying to come up with something else to say. "I have a package I need to send to her. It would be great if you could tell me her address so I can mail it to her there."

"I'm sorry, but I can't give you that information. It's against the rules."

"I understand, but it's really important." I let out a long breath as my stomach twists. "Do you think you could at least give me her phone number?"

"I'm sorry, ma'am, but we're not allowed to give out any personal information."

"I understand. Thank you for your time." I stare at the numbers on the phone box for a long time, unsure what to do next. I could end the call right away, but now that I have someone on the phone, I am determined to get as much information out of her as possible. After a heavy pause, something comes to me. "I'm so sorry, can I ask you one more thing?" I ask and before she can refuse, I continue. "Do you know why Jane left her job?"

"She just left," she says in a tight voice.

"Do you know why?"

The phone goes dead.

I guess she didn't have to answer my questions. But something about her guarded tone has made me even more curious, and as I walk back to the car, where Clark is now stretching sleepily, I wonder how to find out where Jane has gone. She left the hotel, but did she leave Fort Haven too?

Only a guilty person would run.

In a flash, somebody comes to mind. Denise Sanchez, the other friend who turned her back on me. We lived together, the three of us, and at one point we were close. We'd share a bottle of wine after a long day of work at the hotel along with our dreams, and we'd tease each other constantly. My friendship with them evaporated swiftly after I met Brett, but I'm confident Denise and Jane will have stayed in touch even after they both left the hotel. Jane didn't have many other friends that we knew of. So if someone knows where she is, it's Denise.

Maybe she knows even more than that.

CHAPTER 19

The doorbell rings. I drop the wooden spoon into the pan and switch off the stove, putting the scrambled eggs on hold. Nobody ever comes here. We don't even get any post delivered. Could it be the police? Is my time up?

Pulling myself together, I walk over to the door, telling myself that I'm panicking over nothing. Why assume the worst?

"Who is it, Mommy?" Clark asks from the kitchen table, and when there's a knock on the backdoor, he jumps a little. I guess he's picking up on my anxiety.

"Zoe," a woman calls from the other side, "are you in there?"

My shoulders sink with relief. It's Ruth. Before I can open the door, Clark runs to it and pulls it open, throwing himself into her arms.

"Hello, Zoe." Ruth glances around the kitchen curiously. "Why are the blinds closed on such a bright morning?"

"Oh, it was too bright," I lie.

"No, it wasn't," Clark cuts in and I cringe inwardly.

Ruth looks at me, but she says nothing. She knows who the liar is. The truth is that I can't shake the feeling that someone is watching me from the woods. It's beautiful here, but we're so remote, so alone, and increasingly the shadowy branch movements frighten me even when I try to ignore them. I've grown to hate the noises I so often hear in the night: the foxes screeching, the owls crying out to one another, the wind stirring through the leaves. Sometimes it feels like the trees are closing in on me, and the mountains behind them, trapping me and draining the air from my lungs. I never keep the blinds open anymore.

But when Clark sits back down, I open them, just to allay Ruth's curiosity. It feels less frightening when I'm not alone with Clark, anyway.

"We didn't expect you to drop by," I say to her. "What a lovely surprise."

In the entire time we have been staying at the cabin, she's only visited once. We've always gone to her place, even though sometimes I'd have been grateful for the companionship here.

"I'm sorry to show up unannounced. I should have called to let you know." She's smoothing down her dress, a beautiful purple one with rose petals and pleats. It's her favorite, the last gift she got from her husband the Christmas before he died. She wears it at least once a week. "I came to check up on you. I baked a pie." We both look down at her empty hands and she smiles nervously. "I guess old age is catching up with me. I forgot it at the house."

"Well, I'm sure it's delicious, thank you so much anyway." I chew my lip. "It's strange, I didn't hear your car."

"Oh, I came with my bicycle. When my husband was alive, we often rode together."

"Well, we're glad to have you here. Let me make us some coffee. We were just going to have breakfast; would you like some?"

Ruth says she's already eaten, and she sits at the kitchen table, admiring the fresh blue flowers I picked outside. My nerves gradually settling, I serve Clark his eggs on toast and pour coffee for Ruth and me. We make small talk for a little while, both avoiding the real reason why she came here.

Finally, "I miss Clark's visits," she says gently, clutching her steaming mug. "I do understand that you wanted to spend more time with him, but I have a feeling there might be another reason."

Before I respond, I send Clark to the living room to play with the toy train he got from Nora in Disneyland, and when the train sounds make their way to the kitchen, I turn back to Ruth. She's been so kind to both of us, as close to a friend as I can have when I must keep everyone at arm's length. She deserves to know why I'm keeping Clark away from her even though they both need each other.

"Dear girl, are you okay?" Ruth lays a hand on top of mine. Her warmth makes me want to reach out and draw her into a hug. "Something is going on with you; you haven't been yourself for quite some time now. You can tell me anything. I'm a good listener."

"You're right," I say after a moment's silence. "Something is going on." I sigh, and cringe inwardly at the thought of causing her more pain. "Ruth, your son was here." I pause. "To be honest, I feel a little afraid of him because I heard around town about his history, and I know that he's spending a lot of time outside your house."

She slides her hand from mine and closes her eyes. "I had a feeling Luke had something to do with this." Her face sags, and it looks like she has aged a few years in only a matter of seconds. Her shoulders have curled forward and the bags under her eyes seem to have grown darker and heavier. "In a town like Willow Creek, of course word would get to you about his past. I apologize for not saying anything before about him."

"You didn't have to tell me, it's none of my business." As someone who's keeping deeper, darker secrets, I feel a guilty twist in my stomach.

"The thing is, Luke does not feel like my son anymore. I know that's a terrible thing to say, and it must be hard for you to understand. I carried him for nine months and two weeks to be exact. I brought him into this world, and I raised him, but as soon as he became a teenager, he changed beyond recognition. He became a stranger, and he was so terribly unkind to me and to so many others. He was hateful, even, and he made it very clear that he did not love me. He was quite attached to his father, though. And when his father died, he became truly vicious. He took it out on me and his..."

Ruth lowers her eyes, but I already saw the tears in them.

"His brother?" I murmur.

"Daniel was the light of my life. He tried to hold things together when everything was falling apart, and sometimes I wonder if Luke was jealous of my bond with him. Whatever the reason, he was determined to hurt us both. Me, I could cope with his hatred, but I couldn't bear to see what he was doing to Daniel."

She stops talking again and we sit in silence for a moment. I'm about to tell her to stop if it hurts too much, but she's not done yet.

"The boys had a complicated relationship since childhood. It got quite violent at times and Luke usually started it. He spent a lot of time with the wrong crowd, and it got worse and worse. He became violent after his father died, even threatening his brother with weapons, saying he would kill him. I tried to get him help, but nothing worked. I was terrified of him, we both were. Then my worst fears came to pass when they went fishing ten years ago, a year after my husband died. Only Luke returned home."

"Was there an accident?" Tasha said people believe Luke killed his brother, but what if he's innocent? Everyone deserves the benefit of the doubt, even someone as violent and hateful as Ruth is describing.

"I wanted to believe it was an accident, yes. Daniel drowned, at least that's what Luke told us all. His body was found floating..." She inhales sharply. "My son was a strong swimmer. He worked for years as a lifeguard at the local pool, and he loved the water. I've thought about it for so many years, and my heart tells me that Luke—" She wipes her eyes with her sleeve.

"I'm so sorry. If you don't want to talk about it, it's okay." I wipe the tears from my own eyes.

"No, it feels good to talk about it. It's been eating me up inside. Sometimes we must let things out before they poison us."

I wish I could do the same. I wish I could tell her everything, but I can't trust anyone, not even her. Not yet.

"Zoe, please tell me you're not staying away from me because of Luke. He's not a part of my life, not anymore. All he wants is to sell my house and move me into an old age home."

"That's horrible." I shake my head. "You're perfectly capable of living on your own."

"I know, but he wants the money he thinks his father left behind. Don't worry, I'm not going anywhere."

I don't know what to say, and I place my palms on the table and stare at my hands.

"I love taking care of little Clark," Ruth continues. "He makes me feel young again. I would hate to lose the wonderful time we have together. If it's any consolation, Luke left town yesterday and said he never wants to see me again. I guess he finally gave up. Please, continue your life. Go to work. I wouldn't want you to lose your job because of him."

My heart lifts when I hear about Luke's departure, warm relief spreading through my chest, and I smile, nodding at her. "I'll bring Clark by tomorrow."

"Excellent." Ruth pushes back her chair and rises to her feet.

"You're leaving already?" I ask.

She smiles. "I have intruded long enough."

"No, please stay. Have some more coffee."

She agrees, and we spend several pleasant hours together while she tells stories of her childhood and we play with Clark.

When she leaves, I realize that for the first time in a while I haven't felt anxious for hours, I haven't been glancing toward the blinds or pricking up my ears at every little sound from outside. I'm sad to see her go, and I watch from the window as she cycles off, marveling at the impressive fitness she still has at her age. As I clear up the mess of the day, I feel unusually light and cheerful, buoyed up by Ruth's visit and the very welcome news that at least one danger in my life is now gone.

But in the evening, while Clark is watching TV, I step out onto the porch to continue going through my notes and news-paper clippings, and Luke is there.

He's not gone, not at all. He's sitting on the steps, smoking a cigarette.

My heart skips a beat, and I freeze, staring at him. He's wearing jeans and a wrinkled T-shirt that looks like it was once white, but now it's faded to a dirty gray. As usual, his hair is uncombed, and his graying beard sticks out from his face. Seeing him up close, I notice that he has the same amber eyes as his mother.

"W-what are you doing here?" I make a move to step back inside the house, but he pulls out a pack of cigarettes and hands one to me.

"Thanks. I... I don't smoke," I say, feeling completely thrown. Why is he being friendly?

Maybe I'm wrong about him, like others are wrong about me.

"I should really quit." He puts the pack back in his pocket and takes another drag. "These things are the devil. They rob you of your money, and they rob you of your health, but dammit they're addictive little suckers." He looks down at the cigarette in his hand with both love and disdain. "I'm going to stop, though. I've been saying that for years, but I really am." He looks up at me again and his gaze pauses on my face.

My hand still on the doorhandle, I say nothing, utterly confused.

"I like the blonde. It suits you," he says suddenly, his smile a little too wide over his yellow teeth.

Feeling myself go pale, I take a tentative step back into the house, my hands trembling and my heart racing. I shut the door behind me, lock it and lean against it, without uttering a word to him.

He knows.

CHAPTER 20

Tasha takes Clark to a table in a corner of the restaurant and puts coloring pages, puzzles, and books in front of him. He brought his own pencils with him. She agreed to let me work half the day because I had to bring Clark with me. It was either that or I couldn't come at all. After Luke showed up again at the cabin yesterday, I couldn't risk taking Clark to Ruth's. She was upset when I called her to explain, but said she understood.

All night I've been trying hard to dismiss what her son said to me as a random comment, but I can't shake the feeling that he must know something. I had the same color hair when he first saw me. Did he recognize me from the TV or a newspaper? Is that why he's been watching me?

But if so, what's he waiting for? Why hasn't he claimed the reward from Brett's parents, or told the police?

The unshakable reality is that Clark and I are no longer safe here. I hate the thought of leaving the cabin and Willow Creek, and our friendships with Tasha and Ruth. I always knew this day could come, but I'm dreading the thought of being on the road again, of not knowing where we might end up, when we will next see a friendly face. How will I explain it to Clark?

I've been hoping that eventually I can uncover the truth and clear my name, but if Luke knows who I am, he could tell the police.

Shaking me back into the moment, Tasha returns with a plate of eggs, toast, sausages, and pancakes, and puts the food in front of a delighted Clark.

"What do you say, Clark?" I remind him.

"Thank you, Tasha." He pushes aside his drawings and digs in eagerly.

"That's all right, little man." Tasha pats him on the head. "If you need anything else, let us know, okay?"

"Thank you," I mouth to her and walk away from the table. I can keep an eye on Clark the whole time, and I'll also be watching the door in case Luke shows up. It's a slow morning, so at least I can spend some time thinking about what to do next.

Tasha pulls me aside after a little while. "Zoe, talk to me. I know you're going through something."

I want to, so much that it hurts, but I force myself to stay quiet. If Tasha knows what I'm accused of, she would surely feel obligated to turn me in. I like to hope she would believe I'm innocent, but would I, if I were in her shoes?

"Thank you for caring." My gaze moves to Clark. "It means a lot to me."

She squeezes my shoulder. "I'll always be here when you're ready to talk."

I've been so unreliable in recent weeks, and Tasha could easily have fired me and hired someone she can count on. I know some of the staff complain about me, as they have to pick up the slack when I don't show up at work. But Tasha is a good person, and she's helping me without prying into my business. For that, I will forever be grateful.

I'm sitting with Clark during a break at one point, both of us busy completing an ocean puzzle, when Tasha comes to the table with a bright-red train.

"Clark, your Mommy said you like trains." She puts it in front of him. "I hope you'll like this one."

"Thank you! It's really for me?" Clark runs his small hand over the back of the brand-new train.

"If you want it to be." Tasha winks at him and walks away, and I stand up to follow her.

"You didn't have to do that. You've already done so much for us."

"I would do more if you let me." She pauses. "I understand that you're not ready to share your problems with someone else. But you know what, maybe I understand you more than you think." She starts cleaning a table, and I pause by the grandfather clock and watch her. What did she mean?

We work side by side in silence until most of the breakfast crowd trickles out, and in another lull Tasha continues the conversation as if we never stopped.

"I was wrong," she says. "I don't know what you're going through. It was wrong of me to imply that I did, I'm sorry about that."

"It's fine," I respond, but I wish she would continue. A part of me is yearning to know her more.

As if reading my mind, she continues, "You might not know this, but I was once a single mother. Jack has not always been in my life."

"Really?" I didn't know that. Whenever he comes to Lemon with the twins, Jack treats them like his own. I never once suspected he was not their biological father. "I—"

"My late husband died a month after we got married, and I was pregnant. We were already struggling financially before his death, and when he died, I had nothing to give my kids. The little money he left me went toward funeral expenses and hospital bills." She sighs. "I struggled for a long time as a single parent. I stayed in a shelter once and worked jobs I hated. Then Jack came along and helped me rescue myself."

"I'm so sorry." Without giving it much thought, I draw her into my arms. She's as surprised by the hug as I am, and after an awkward moment, I pull back again, but she smiles.

"The one thing that helped me through rough times was talking to people who care."

I nod and look down at my feet. She's waiting for me to open up as well, but it doesn't happen. It can't. When some more customers enter, I hurry to them, grateful for the distraction. I hope she won't pursue the topic later.

The customers are two women in their twenties, and one of them is staring at me in a way that makes me shift with discomfort. She should be flipping through the menu, but instead, her eyes are fixed on my face. I push back my shoulders and put on my brightest smile. "What can I get you?"

"Oh, sorry." The woman peels her gaze from my face and reaches for the menu. They order pancakes, sausages, and orange juice.

I hurry away from the table, my stomach churning. I'm used to people lowering their voices when I walk by, and I just know they are whispering behind my back about the widow living in a cabin in the woods, but this time is different. The woman is looking at me as if she knows me from somewhere and is trying to figure it out.

It's nothing, I tell myself. *Hold your nerve.*

When I serve their food, she gives me a sweet smile and thanks me.

"I was wondering," she says before I leave them. "Do I know you? I'm really good with faces and you look familiar. I feel like we've seen each other before."

"No." A nervous laugh spills from my lips as blood rushes to my brain. "I mean, I don't think so." I force a smile. "Is there anything else I can bring you?"

The two women shake their heads and I hurry off, almost tripping.

"Are you all right?" Tasha asks me at the bar.

"No." It's probably the most honest I've ever been with her. "Can we talk in private?"

Tasha suggests we go to her office, but I don't want to let Clark out of my sight, so we take a seat at one of the empty tables. Her eyes are filled with questions and her hands are clasped on the table. "You can tell me anything."

"No, I can't. I'm sorry. I'm so grateful for everything you've done for me, but I can't work here... not anymore."

That woman might watch the news tonight and see me on TV. If she figures out who I am, she will return with the cops. Even if she doesn't, surely it's only a matter of time before Luke stops tormenting me and turns me in. Maybe he wants money, but I don't have any to give him.

"Oh, I don't understand. I thought you liked it here." Tasha narrows her eyes. "Did you find another job?"

I shake my head. The thought of having to look for another job elsewhere and start from scratch makes my insides burn with anxiety. Tasha only wants to help me and she's not pushing to know who I am or where I came from. Another employer might want to know more, and they will surely not be as understanding as she is. But as much as I hate it, in the next few days, we will have to leave town and go to another place where no one knows me. It was a mistake to stay in Willow Creek for this long. I gaze at Clark and tears fill my eyes. I hate to drag him away again from the place he has come to know as home.

"Is it about what I said?" She places a hand on mine. "I hope I didn't overstep. I only want to understand you more so I can help better."

"You don't want to know me, Tasha," I say to her. "I'm too much trouble. Thank you for what you've done. I'll never forget it. And I'm sorry to leave you like this." I squeeze her hand tight, wishing I didn't have to lose yet another friendship.

Before letting us go, Tasha packs up some lunch for us on the house and gives it to me with confusion still in her eyes, and five minutes later, Clark and I are back in the car. He's as confused as Tasha was about us leaving so soon. He doesn't say a word to me all the way to the cabin. I try everything, even ask him to sing with me to the radio, but I get nothing back.

"I'm sorry we had to leave, but, baby, sometimes parents have to make decisions that kids don't understand."

Still, he says nothing.

The moment the car stops in front of the cabin, Clark gets out and slams the door hard. I watch him stomp toward the front door, clutching his train. I follow behind him, feeling slow, heavy, and like I'm wading through a sea of mud. My eyes dart between the trees' swaying branches, and I try to calm myself by tuning into the sound of birds chirping alongside the soft thud of my son's sneakers on the wooden porch steps.

A beautiful butterfly suddenly flutters by, and I pause to watch it before I continue. Its wings are a bright-orange color pattern with black markings in the center. I stare after it until it lands on a little blue flower. Peeling my gaze away from it, I swallow hard, telling myself I'm just being silly. But despite the tranquility and peace here, I feel a ripple of unease running down my spine as I climb the steps. The surrounding beauty feels like some kind of setup, as if I'm stepping into a world where nothing is what it seems and everything is a facade: the cabin, the woods, the trees, the sounds of the birds, everything.

Then, before I can unlock the door, I notice a newspaper clipping on the porch underneath a potted plant, one end fluttering in the wind like a bird's wing. My pulse races as I open the door quickly and usher Clark into the house, telling myself it's just a piece of trash. But when I go back to pick it up, my mouth goes dry.

Brett's widow is still wanted for murder, screams the headline.

I've seen this clipping before. But what is it doing outside?

Then I unfold it, and for a moment it's as if time has paused and the world has stopped spinning, except for the sound of my heart pounding in my ears.

My face is circled in blood-red marker.

"One more time, Mommy," Clark begs when I finish reading his favorite bedtime story, *The Goose Prince*, a second time. I'm exhausted, and still reeling after what I saw on the porch, but I've triple-checked all the locks, and I need to keep my wits about me and be there for Clark.

I give in. "One last time. Then you have to sleep, okay?"

He gives me a bright smile and curls up next to me on the bed.

I'm lying next to him and reading his story, but my mind is drifting to the newspaper clipping. I went through my papers, and I didn't find it. But it was definitely one of the ones I printed out, so someone must have come into the cabin and taken it, along with the red pen I used to make notes.

Was it Luke?

If so, how did he get in? There are no other signs that anyone was inside. And what is he planning on doing next?

There's another possible explanation, which is equally frightening to me right now. Did I circle it myself, in my sleep last night, and wandered outside with it? It seems crazy, but I have woken up sleepwalking before, rifling anxiously through those articles.

If so, what other things have I done in my sleep?

When Clark has drifted off, I go into the living room and sit in front of the unlit fireplace, thinking about what to do next. My mind is yelling for me to run now, this very night, to pack our bags, take Clark and get out of Willow Creek, the town I have come to love.

But I can't be impulsive. I can't run in a blind panic without knowing where I'm going. I need to calm down enough to come up with a plan. Until I've done that, I will just have to hide out here for a little longer, but with all my wits about me, ready to go the minute things turn sour.

CHAPTER 21

We have stayed indoors for three days with nothing out of the ordinary happening, but we're running out of food. I have no choice but to get out there again and stock up, even if I'm still nervous about being recognized.

Clark is overjoyed when I tell him about our trip to the grocery store, and I stuff a bag with canned foods, rice and pasta, and anything with a long shelf life that we can take on the road with us when we go.

We're at the cash register when Clark decides to be difficult. He's angry because I refuse to buy him a superhero toy, but we can't waste the little money we have, not when I don't have a job to bring in more. I place my hand on his head and try to calm him down, to prevent him from throwing a tantrum. He has been doing that a lot lately, as the stress of being cooped up inside the cabin has gotten to him. I understand; I'm struggling as well.

Clark knows something is wrong, and he knows I'm afraid. On more than one occasion, he woke up in the middle of the night to find me sleepwalking and looking out the window or saw me jump when he walked into the room.

"How about I get you this instead." I reach for a less expensive toy race car. People are watching; we need to get out as soon as possible.

At first, he protests, then he scowls in defeat. "Fine," he mumbles and folds his arms. "Can I get the other toy next time?"

"Maybe." Maybe one day I'll be able to buy him what he wants, but right now I cannot spend fifty dollars on a toy. In any other circumstance, I would have words with him about his behavior, but I can't blame him for acting out when he's been cooped up for so long. I toss the new toy into the cart and wheel it forward to the checkout.

Out of the corner of my eye, I try not to stare at the newspaper on the stand with a small photo of me in one corner of the cover.

I pay quickly and rush Clark back to the car, but as soon as I shut his door, that familiar feeling of being watched trickles down my spine. I can feel goosebumps forming on my skin and I freeze in place, not daring to turn around, afraid of what I might see.

Then I take a deep breath, and look.

It's Luke.

Of course.

My body is tight with tension as our eyes meet from across the parking lot. He's inside his pickup truck, staring directly at me.

What do you want from me, I want to scream.

I wish I could charge toward him and demand he stay away from us, but I need to keep my distance. I'll be gone soon enough, I just need to pluck up the courage to explain to Clark and choose where to go next.

My eyes are still on Luke as I slide behind the wheel, palms slick against the old leather.

Clark says something from the backseat, but I cannot hear

his words. Through the rushing in my ears, his voice sounds distant. I watch as Luke drives away, his truck disappearing around the corner. I let out the breath I was holding and rest my forehead on the steering wheel.

"Are you okay, Mommy?" Clark asks and I swallow hard before I turn to look at him.

"Mommy is just tired, baby."

"Is it because you don't sleep?" he asks. "In the night, you went to the window again. I saw you."

He must have seen me walking in my sleep again.

"I'm sorry that I woke you," I say as lightly as I can manage.

"It's okay, Mommy. Don't feel bad. You should drink warm milk. It will make you sleepy."

"That's a good idea. Maybe I will." I ignore the tears threatening to spill over. I haven't cried in a long time, but everything is just getting too much for me now. Without another word, I pull out of the parking lot and drive back to the cabin, glancing in the rearview mirror every few seconds to make sure Luke is not behind us.

My phone rings. It's Ruth, and she has already called several times today. I don't pick up again, because lately our phone conversations are always about the same thing, and I can't give her the answer she wants. She's still desperate to see Clark, and she's trying to convince me that we have nothing to fear from Luke.

I wish I could believe her.

On our way to the cabin, we drop by a payphone, and I dial the number I found in the Fort Haven online directory. When the phone starts ringing, nervous butterflies erupt in my belly. I haven't spoken to Denise for years. After she stopped working at the hotel, I tried to call her several times, but she never answered, and not long after, her number went out of service, so I gave up and went on with my life.

I'm calling her mother's house phone. They were always

close, and before we moved in together, Denise used to live with her. The phone rings five times with no answer, and I'm just about to hang up when someone picks up.

"Hello?" The woman has a raspy, tired voice. "Who is this?"

"I'm sorry to disturb you. I'm an old friend of Denise. I'm unable to reach her on her cell. Is she in?"

Silence.

"What do you want from my daughter?" She sounds both curious and annoyed.

I rub the back of my neck. "We haven't spoken for a while and I just wanted to get in touch."

"I'm sorry." She cuts me off. "You can't speak to my daughter."

My heart sinks. Denise isn't there. I knew she had moved back in with her mother, but that was a long time ago. "Would you mind giving me her new cell phone number? The one I have no longer exists."

"I-I'm sorry to have to tell you this, but Denise is dead."

"She's what?" I gasp. "How? When?" I sink against the dirty glass of the cubicle, and my eyes grow blurry as I stare at my car outside.

"A year and four months." Her voice is barely audible. "She was a good girl."

"Yes," I say, my voice cracking. "Yes, she was a wonderful person. How did she... How did she die?"

I don't want to put the woman through any more pain, but I need to know.

"The cops said she killed herself. It all went wrong when she was working at that awful hotel. I know something happened to her there, but she would never tell me. I think they treated her badly. I think they hurt my baby. And now she's dead."

"Oh my God," I murmur, my fingertips touching my lips and my eyes filling with tears.

After the call, I stand in stunned silence for a while. My head is spinning so fast that it's impossible to make sense of it all.

I can't believe Denise is gone.

Could it be true?

There were rumors of harassment at the hotel, of a toxic working environment brushed over by management. Jane hinted at it when she came to work for Brett and me, and I was sure Brett would ask her to leave given her obvious hostility toward us.

What if Brett knew about the harassment, and he let her stay because he felt guilty?

Was what happened there bad enough to drive Denise to suicide?

CHAPTER 22

Clark is eating his fries and roasted chicken while I move my food around the plate. The news about Denise's death has hit me hard, and I'm too preoccupied to eat. Her mother said she died sixteen months ago, so her death must have happened around the time Brett was diagnosed with cancer.

Why would she kill herself? She was struggling financially, but she was optimistic that things would get better. She was one of the most positive people I knew. Denise was the kind of person who spent her free time reading motivational books and had affirmations plastered to the inside of her staff locker. Even though, like me, she didn't finish school, she was determined to create a better life for herself. Working as a maid was only temporary; her dream was to start her own wire-wrapped jewelry business. She showed me a few pieces. She was talented.

Now it's all over. She died with her dream inside of her.

Is the harassment the reason why she cut off contact with me? Did something happen at the hotel, and she wouldn't tell me because I married into the family business? I had become a Wilton; maybe she blamed me along with them. When I told

Jane and Denise that I was engaged, Jane told me that she didn't trust the Wiltons. But I dismissed it as jealousy.

After telling me about her daughter's death, Denise's mother was so distraught that she couldn't speak anymore, and I didn't get any of the answers I needed. Breaking my own rule, when we got to the cabin, I used my own phone to leave her a message telling her how sorry I was to hear about Denise, and that I would call her again in a few days to check up on her. I didn't tell her my name, of course.

I wipe away the tears before Clark sees them. I'm tired of him asking me if I'm okay. I'm tired of making him feel like he has to take care of me.

I need to get my life back before I ruin his completely.

The doorbell rings while Clark and I are watching TV after dinner. "Go to our room and put on your pajamas," I say. "I'll come and join you soon."

When Clark is in the room, I go to the front door and peer through the peephole.

It's Luke.

"I know you're in there," he says in a slurred voice. Something hard hits the door and I jump back as I hear glass shattering. Probably an empty beer bottle. Like last time he showed up, I didn't hear his truck. He must have parked a distance away and walked. "That's my cabin you're living in. You can't keep me out," he continues when I don't respond.

I cover my mouth with my hand. That's it. I'm living in his mother's cabin, and he must have lived here first. Of course he wants me gone.

"You don't have to be afraid of me," he continues. "I just want to talk, that's all. I've been told I'm a pretty good listener, and you always seem like you have a lot on your mind. I think you need to open up."

While I'm struggling to figure out what to do, the distant sound of police sirens cuts through the silence around me.

He called the cops on me.

It's game over.

Clark appears in the living room, and I sense his presence before I see him. I turn around and run to him, clutching him to my body. "Mommy loves you. I love you so much." I press my lips on top of his head. "Please forgive me."

"Is something bad happening, Mommy?"

"I don't know," I say, then I bite hard into my bottom lip.

I wait inside the cabin as the sirens grow louder. I'm afraid to open the door.

These might be the last moments I have with my son.

And then, raised voices, followed by a gunshot.

Someone starts shouting; it's Luke's voice.

Confusion clouds my mind. The only thing I can do is hold on tighter to Clark, waiting for the police to break down the door. But they don't. After what seems like forever, there's only a knock.

"Miss, this is the police, are you all right in there?" It's a woman's voice.

I blink away tears. "Yes." My voice is too low for the police-woman to hear me. I try again. "I'm fine."

The policewoman orders me to open the door. I'm terrified, but I do as I'm told, clutching Clark's hand.

The woman looks from me to him. "Are you or your son hurt?"

I shake my head as my eyes gaze past her shoulders to see Luke's figure inside the police car. They came for him, not me.

After asking me a couple of questions, they all leave and drive away.

I'm still free, but for how long? Will Luke tell them what I suspect he knows?

CHAPTER 23

I'm shaken to the core after the police leave, and I pour myself a glass of white wine, my hand shaking. When I turn around, my heart sinks as I see Clark's damp, red eyes. I can tell the poor boy was terrified by everything that had just happened, but he also looks very sleepy.

I draw him to me and squeeze him. "You don't have to be scared, baby. I won't let anything happen to you." Clark tightens his arms around me, and we hold each other for a long time. I give him a watery smile when we pull apart. "Mommy will always be here for you."

He nods, then he walks to the bedroom and closes the door.

I sink into a chair at the kitchen table, gulping down my wine. How long until they return to get me?

Blood drains from my face at the sound of a car nearing the house. They're back already. Luke must have told them who I am on the way to the station, and now they have returned before I can run.

Why on earth did I wait?

Everything is happening too fast.

I'm still frozen at the table when the doorbell rings.

"Open the door, Zoe." It's Ruth, thank God, not the police. What is she doing here? Did she hear about Luke already?

The moment I get to my feet, a wave of dizziness washes over me, getting worse with each step. I drank that wine far too quickly. Before I can open it, Clark runs into the room, calling out for Mrs. Foster. The joy in his voice, the laughter in his eyes, make my heart hurt. He opens the door before I can and Ruth steps in. I'm shocked by how pale she is, and the wrinkles on her face look like they have deepened even further.

Ruth crouches down and hugs Clark for longer than usual, putting her chin on the top of his head and closing her eyes. Then she lets go and puts both hands on his shoulders.

"I need you to go to bed now. It's late. I'm sorry if I woke you."

"The police were here," Clark blurts out. "They took the bad man away."

"Is that so?" Ruth glances at me, then back at him. "I need to have a quick word with your mother. Be a good boy and go to bed."

Clark's face falls. "Can I visit you tomorrow?"

I pull myself together and step in to rescue Ruth. "Clark, it's very late and it's time for bed. Come on now." I take his hand and return him to the bedroom.

When I come back to the living room, I find Ruth sitting on the couch, her back straight and her hands clasped in her lap. She doesn't look at me when I enter, staring straight ahead at the blank TV screen. I sit next to her, and she still doesn't look at me.

"Luke was here, and then the police showed up," I say quickly, because she deserves to know, although judging by the expression on her face I think she already does.

"I'm aware of that," she says, still not meeting my eyes. "He told me he was headed here."

"Luke came to see you before he—?"

"No, he came to threaten me. He kept talking about you too, and I was afraid he might harm you. He had a gun, so I felt it best to call the police."

"Thank you." It must have been hard for her to call the cops on her own son. "This was his cabin, wasn't it?" I ask.

"It was the family cabin. He only thought it belonged to him; he thinks everything belongs to him." She pauses, taking a deep breath. "Zoe, I'm so sorry, but I have to ask you to leave."

"I don't understand." Confusion washes over me as I look at the woman who has been so kind to me over the last months.

"I think you do." Her voice is low as she finally looks at me. "Meghan Wilton, that's your name, right? When I gave you a place to stay, you didn't tell me you're wanted for murder."

I take a shuddering breath in and place my head in my hands. I can't find it in me to deny it. I've lied to her long enough.

We sit in silence for a little while, and it occurs to me that Ruth did not tell the police about me. Maybe she's giving me a chance to get away first. I feel so broken by her kindness, and by the gnawing guilt I feel for betraying her trust.

"I'm not one to watch a lot of TV, but lately, without Clark to look after, I've had a lot of time on my hands, and I saw a photo of you on the news. You look very different now... almost like someone else, but the woman in the paper has this same heart-shaped birthmark." She places a hand on my shoulder and her thumb brushes the birthmark on my collarbone. "That's how I saw it. I didn't want to believe it was you, but tonight, when Luke kept referring to you as Meghan in his angry rambling, I just knew."

When I don't respond, she lifts a lock of my hair. "I know your natural hair color is not blonde. I've seen the dark roots a couple of times." I close my eyes, still hidden under my hands.

"They said the fugitive woman also had a four-year-old son who must be five now."

I open my lips to speak, but no words come out, and slowly I raise my head. "It's not what you think, Ruth. I loved my husband. He was sick and—"

"You don't have to explain anything to me. I just came to tell you that I need you to leave by tomorrow night. I have come to be very fond of your son, and for his sake, I won't tell the police. But I need you to go now. Leave the key under the mat."

"Thank you." I blink away tears. "Thank you for everything. But it's not what you think. I didn't... I'm not a—"

She raises a hand and gets to her feet. "Like I said, I don't want to know anything more. Take your boy and run. Murderers are not welcome in my home or in my life." Tears are glistening on her cheeks.

Ruth asks if she can say goodbye to Clark, and we go together to the bedroom. My little boy is so sleepy and completely unaware that his life is going to be turned upside down once again. Ruth stares at him for a long time, then kisses his forehead.

"Sweet dreams, little one," she says sadly.

As soon as Ruth leaves, I take a few minutes to get my head straight. I don't want to disturb Clark again, but I'd rather not wait until morning to leave, not now that Ruth has confirmed Luke knows who I am.

In the end, I pack our bags and load them into the car so we can leave first thing in the morning, and text Tasha to say goodbye. The moon is bright this evening, a blazing white circle above the trees.

Now that we're leaving, I don't feel afraid of the forest, I don't feel trapped. I only know I'm going to miss this place, our little refuge. I doubt we'll find somewhere this perfect again.

I finish the bottle of wine and go to bed, falling asleep immediately, too exhausted even to dream.

CHAPTER 24

Gently shaking Clark awake early the next day, I tell him we're leaving the cabin and try to frame it as another adventure, but he starts crying. My attempts to comfort him fail as he pushes me away and locks himself in the bathroom. I feel as though I'm losing both my son and my sanity. He's all I have, and I cannot afford for him to slip through my fingers. He thought we had found a home. He had come to see Ruth as his grandmother. And now he just found out he might never see her again. It's too much for a little boy to deal with.

But sometimes life can be cruel and you either crumble or you do what you have to do. You survive.

I give Clark the time he needs, but I'm pacing anxiously up and down in the living room. When he finally joins me, I bring him into my arms and hold him tight, willing myself to be strong.

"Are you ready for another adventure, Superboy?" I ask, letting him go. "We're leaving now. We'll have breakfast on the road."

"Okay," he says, but his voice is empty of emotion.

After scanning the cabin one final time, I write Ruth a letter

to thank her for all she's done. On the other side of the page, Clark
draws a picture of a little boy carrying a toy train. Then, without
asking me where we are going next, he goes to get into the car.

I sit behind the steering wheel, willing myself to start the car.
But I have no idea where we'll go. Should we move to another
small town or a big city? Wherever we go, I don't think we will
find as good a hiding place as the cabin and I doubt we will find
another Mrs. Foster waiting for us at our next destination.

I look back at my son, who is just staring back at our cabin,
and I suspect he's trying to make sure he remembers it when
we're gone. I can't bear what this is doing to him, and I know
that, as long as I'm not free, Clark isn't either. He will always be
looking over his shoulder, just like me. He won't have the luxury
of a normal life like other kids. He will be scarred by every bad
decision I make, and the consequences will suffocate both of us.

Will he blame me one day for the choices I'm making
right now?

Giving myself a shake, I make a snap decision. We will hide
out in Rogersville for now. It's only an hour away and we had
stayed in a motel there for a few days before choosing to settle in
Willow Creek.

But just as I'm about to drive off, I hear another car coming
toward us, and I wonder if it's Ruth. Has she changed her
mind?

Is it the police, am I too late?

To my relief, it's Tasha. Surprised to see her, I jump out of
the car and go to hug her. It's so early, she must have been determined to see me before I leave.

"Hi." I hesitate, unsure what to say.

"I'm sorry, I know you said you have to leave urgently," she
says. "I won't be long."

"No, it's fine. I've got a minute." I stand awkwardly as she waves at Clark through the car window. "I'm surprised to see you," I say.

She pinches the skin at her throat nervously. "Zoe, I'm worried about you. After the way you left the restaurant the other day, and then your text last night, I needed to make sure that you're okay."

I feel suddenly cold. Will Ruth tell her about me?

"So, this is where you've been living?" She takes in the cabin, her gaze resting on a cracked window.

I nod. "We're going away now."

"But not for good, right?" When I say nothing, her eyes widen. "Zoe, you can't do that. Clark is so happy here. I know how moving around can affect a child. My kids hated being moved around."

"I don't have a choice." I run a jerky hand through my hair. "We need to go now."

"Why, did Ruth ask you to leave?"

When I don't respond, she sighs. "Why don't you come and stay with us until you figure out what to do next? We have a guest house. You and Clark can stay there."

"I don't want to get you in trouble." As soon as the words leave my mouth, I realize my mistake.

She's only quiet for a moment, then she squeezes my arm. "Don't worry about that. Friends are there for each other."

But we can't be friends. She doesn't know the real me, and if she did, she would run a mile. I still haven't recovered from the look of betrayal in Ruth's eyes. I can't bear the thought of Tasha looking at me like that, too.

"Tasha, you have no idea how much your offer means to me, but I can't accept it."

"All right, then," she says sadly. "Then take this, okay?" She reaches into her purse and hands me an envelope. "It's your payment for this month and a little extra from me. Hopefully it'll cover you while you find a new place to stay."

I open the envelope and look at the cash inside. "This is too much. Why are you doing this?" I ask, completely taken aback. There's an extra two hundred dollars.

"Because when I was in a tough situation, many people helped me out along the way, and I'm paying it forward. I care about you and your son, and I want you to be safe. But please, let me know where you're going. You have my number, so call me when you need anything, or if you change your mind about coming to stay with us."

"Thank you, Tasha. Thank you so much." I want to refuse the extra money, to give it back, but I really need it. I'm touched deeply by her generosity, and once again my chest hurts at the thought of losing another friend.

Before she gets back in her car, Tasha hugs me tight and when she lets go, there are tears in both our eyes.

"Take care of yourself," she whispers. "And if you need anything, call me. Anything at all."

With that, Clark and I are on the road once again. As we leave the town behind us, I keep waiting for the sound of sirens, but I hear nothing. In my heart, though, I know it's only a matter of time.

CHAPTER 25

I slide the coins into the motel vending machine and Clark chooses corn chips for his treat. I feel like a terrible mother for feeding him junk food again, but I need him to be happy and if that means buying him snacks, then for now, that's what I'll do.

I paid for our three-night stay at the Midnight Motel in cash. I'm relieved to find that it's really quiet; there are ten rooms in the motel and only two are occupied. The owner hands me the key with barely a glance at my face, and as we walk down the scuffed carpet to our room, I clutch Clark's hand, as if he's the one comforting me.

In the beginning, Clark used to get excited every time we entered a new place, but this time, he doesn't even look at the room. Instead, he walks slowly to a rickety chair by the window and sits down, then he pushes his hand into the bag of chips. He hasn't said much during our drive to the motel. He's still hurting, and I wish I had the power to erase his pain.

As we drove through the early morning light, I told Clark we are like nomads, never staying in one place for too long because we crave adventure. He simply shrugged his shoulders and stared out of the window. How long can I still fool him into believing this is how normal people live?

I'm about to draw the curtains to let in the sunshine, but I decide against it. We're on the first floor; why risk someone looking inside and recognizing me?

"It's too dark, Mommy." Clark looks up from his chips. "Can you open the curtains?"

"Let's keep them closed for a little while, okay?"

"No," he demands. "I want to read my book."

"All right." I open the heavier curtain just enough to brighten the room, but the sheer curtain underneath stays in place. Satisfied, Clark moves over to the bed, puts his chips next to him, and opens the fairy-tale book he had been flipping through in the car.

My phone rings inside my purse, and I hold my breath. The only people who call me are Ruth and Tasha, but the caller ID is hidden. I stare at the phone until it stops ringing and beeps to signal that the person has left a message, and I listen to it right away.

"Hello, this is Mandy Sanchez, Denise's mother. Please call me back." She sounds like she's in a hurry.

While Clark is still leafing through his book, I sneak outside to return the call in the corridor.

"Who are you?" Mrs. Sanchez asks, and her question takes me by surprise.

"Denise's friend," I tell her again.

"In that case," she says slowly, "can you help get justice for my daughter? She didn't deserve to die that way. They say she jumped out of the window of our apartment, but I just don't believe it."

The image of my friend lying twisted on a pavement burns into my mind. Poor, lovely Denise. She had so much of life still ahead of her. "I don't know if I can help, but I'll try," I say even though I have no idea how. Tears are clogging my throat now and Clark is at the door, eyeing me curiously.

"Please, she was all I had. I dream about her every night. Someone needs to pay for what happened to her."

"I know," I say. "I hope they will." I don't know what I can do for Denise's mother. But I need to say something to her to make her feel like someone else cares. If only I knew exactly what happened to Denise and the others.

I did know that Nora was verbally abusive to the maids; I experienced it myself.

What else is she capable of?

"Thank you," she says. "Thank you so much."

"You're welcome." I pause. "Is there anything else you can tell me about what happened to Denise? Anything important that she said to you?"

Mrs. Sanchez sniffs. "She wouldn't talk about it. But she had a friend, who called me a few months ago. She also said she will help us get justice, but I haven't heard anything from her since. I don't know what to do; I need all the help I can get."

I return to the room and I pull out my notepad. "Did this friend tell you how she intends to do that?"

"She told me she was starting a secret group on Facebook where previous employees from the Black Oyster Hotel will post their stories, and then she will take everything to the police."

Holding my pen over the page, I ask, "Do you have her name and number? Maybe I can contact her for more information."

"Jane something. I forgot to ask for her number, but she said she will keep in touch. But it's been months now. When you called me, you gave me hope again."

Jane. Was she one of the employees who were harassed? I helped her and Denise get jobs at the Black Oyster. Did they blame me for whatever happened to them there? Maybe they even thought I knew, but I did nothing about it.

"I will go to the police station again too," Mrs. Sanchez cuts through my thoughts. "I'm going to look for Denise's journals and give them to the police."

"That's good." I say slowly, my mind whirling. "That's a good idea."

"Denise used to love journaling," she continues. "She said it helped free her mind. I hope her words will lead the police in the right direction."

When I end the call after promising Mrs. Sanchez that I'll keep her updated, I write down everything she shared with me, trying to process what I heard. It's a shame she didn't know the name of the secret Facebook group Jane was going to start.

"I'm still hungry, Mommy," Clark says and I pull myself out of my haze and make us tomato sandwiches. We eat in front of the TV without switching it on; I don't want to make the mistake of falling asleep with the TV on and waking up to find him seeing my face on the news. So even though Clark begs to watch cartoons, the TV stays off.

After our meal, I read him his favorite books until he grows drowsy and falls asleep.

I'm about to close the curtains again when I catch sight of a police car parked in front of the motel.

In a panic, I check to see if the door is closed. Where can I go? I'm trapped.

Overwhelmed with sadness, I glance at my son. I've failed him.

I watch through the curtains, my heart pounding hard, but the police car remains in the parking lot for half an hour, and no one gets in or out. I keep expecting them to knock on the door, but they don't.

The urge to use the bathroom forces me to walk away from the window, and when I return, the car is gone.

For a split second, I consider calling Tasha to ask if the offer to stay in her guest house still stands, but then I remind myself that if Luke tells the police who I am, they are sure to question her very quickly.

I lie next to Clark and pull him into my arms, protecting him the only way I know how.

CHAPTER 26

When I open my eyes in the morning, the events of the past few days replay in my head, shaking me awake. The room is glowing with light spilling in through the orange curtains and the faint smell of the musty carpet fills my nostrils. I can hear traffic in the distance, a car door slamming, and the muffled sound of a TV in the next room making its way through the thin walls. Clark is still asleep next to me. His breathing is easy and steady, but mine is heavy, as if I just woke up from a nightmare.

Since I spoke to Mrs. Sanchez three days ago, I can't stop thinking about whether Jane could have been the one who killed Brett. If she thinks his family swept a terrible harassment problem at the hotel under the mat, and she had been hurt by it herself, then she must have really hated him. He was already dying, but perhaps she was angry enough that she couldn't wait any longer. After all, she was definitely in the house that night.

It's possible that she saw me struggling with the decision to inject Brett before I left the room. Then she could have done the unthinkable herself, seeing it as an opportunity to get revenge on us both. In her mind, I'm the friend who betrayed her, by marrying into the family who were behind her suffering.

And now she's opening a secret Facebook group, hoping to see the rest of the Wilton family go down.

I sit up, pushing the covers off my body, and swing my legs over the side of the bed. Then I walk to the window, parting the curtains in the middle. It's a beautiful day. Above the trees and mountains, the sky is a clear, pearly blue, and the wind fills the room with the scent of pine and crushed wildflowers. A blue jay makes its way through the branches of a tree, darting in and out of the shadows. But I'm not in the right state of mind to enjoy the view; my stomach is filled with churning anxiety and burning questions.

I look back on those golden days with Jane and Denise in our little apartment. I never could have imagined it would come to this, with one of us dead, one on the run, and one who I suspect killed my husband.

The question is, where is Jane now? I've escaped the punishment she tried to give me by running away. Would she give up on her plan for revenge after she's already taken it so far?

As I let the curtain fall again and watch my sleeping son, I remember the day Jane told me about Willow Creek, how she said she would return one day in her later years to settle there.

What if she already did?

What if she found me?

For all I know it was her who I felt was watching me from the woods, all that time. Perhaps it was her who circled my face on that article, not Luke, and not me.

But if that's the case, wouldn't she have told the police where I am?

Unless she wants to taunt me first. Does she eventually want me to die, like Brett did?

I can't believe how dark my thoughts are growing, but my life has changed incomparably, and it feels sometimes like I'm cursed, just waiting for the next terrible thing to unfold.

The only good thing in my life, the only thing keeping me going, is my son.

As I watch him, Clark opens his puffy eyes and stretches, then his mouth quirks into a grin. "Mommy," he yawns. "Can we eat pancakes for breakfast, please?"

Too emotional to speak, I nod and ruffle his hair. He has asked me the same question for two days in a row and today I don't have it in me to deny him something that would make him feel normal and happy. "We can't make pancakes here, baby, but I saw a restaurant not far away."

I'm helping him get dressed when another thought strikes me.

Given that Willow Creek is a small town, and they are roughly the same age, what if Jane and Luke knew each other?

CHAPTER 27

Located only five minutes' drive away, the Oak Diner has seen better days, but its service and food are good. It's nondescript and sits between a car wash and a pizza joint. Pictures of long-gone family members, according to the sign above them, hang along one wall, and red and white checkered tablecloths are draped over the tables. The place is mostly empty except for an inky-haired waitress wearing a blue-and-white 1950s-style dress, and two middle-aged men drinking beer for breakfast.

The low "yummy" noises Clark is making while finishing up his pancakes and bacon warm my heart. Taking him out for breakfast was a good idea. For a while, I feel slightly calmer, sipping my coffee and nibbling my food.

But now my eyes are glued on the small propped-up TV. It's on mute, and thankfully Clark is sitting with his back to it, otherwise he would have seen his father's face on the news.

"Mommy, I want more breakfast please," he says, holding up his dull metal fork just as a photo of him is shown on the screen. I stare at him, my head spinning. Then I shake myself into action and jump up from my chair.

"We need to leave." It's a good thing we're seated not too far from the door. We'll be able to make a quick escape before the people in the diner recognize one of us.

"But I don't want to go," Clark whines, biting on a piece of crunchy bacon. "I want to finish my bacon and have more pancakes."

"Sweetie, that's your last piece. You can eat it on the way to the car."

While he continues to chew his food, ignoring my request, I reach into my purse for money, and I drop a twenty-dollar bill next to the vase of fake red roses.

"Why do we always leave early?" Clark juts out his bottom lip.

"I'm sorry, but sweetheart, sometimes we have to do things we don't want to do. And we stayed long enough for you to finish your food." I search my brain for something to comfort him. "We can play some more games at the motel."

"I hate the motel. It's stupid."

"Don't say that. It's all part of our big adventure." I reach for his arm again and pull him out of his chair, still looking at the TV out of the corner of my eye. He continues to fight me off, and I'm growing desperate.

"Clark, please, do what Mommy is telling you. I'll explain later," I say, my voice tense. I'm terrified that we're drawing attention from the other diners, and I'm gripping his arm too tight as I try to pull him out of there with me.

"I hate you." He pushes away from me, and storms out of the restaurant.

It's amazing how crushing a few simple words can be.

During the drive back to the motel, Clark refuses to speak to me and it kills me inside, but I understand. I just hope that one day he'll forgive me for all this turbulence, for the lack of stability, the loneliness, the anxiety I'm passing onto him. He barely says anything for the rest of the day, and at bedtime, he goes to bed without a fight. He's hurting and I don't know how to help him heal without telling him the truth.

As soon as he's asleep, I switch on the TV and slide to the edge of the bed, blocking his view in case he opens his eyes.

"I'm sorry, Mommy." Clark's sleepy voice makes me jump. "Sorry I was bad to you."

I switch the TV off again and crawl back into bed next to him.

"You're not bad, Superboy." I kiss him on his warm cheek. "I'm sorry for taking you out of the restaurant before you finished eating."

Honestly, we could have stayed a little longer. With my blonde hair and his growth spurt, we don't look very similar to the pictures on the news. But I panicked and the only thing on my mind was to flee even though that probably drew even more attention to us. Running is an automatic reaction, and it has kept us safe for this long.

"I love you, Mommy," he whispers and draws closer to me, burying his face in my chest like he used to when he was a baby.

"I love you much more." I close my eyes and rest my chin on the top of his head. "Forever together?" I ask.

"Forever and ever," he whispers.

Warmth spreads through my chest, soothing some of the cracks on my heart. But more cracks are still appearing, one at a time, day by day.

I wish I could watch TV again, but I can't risk it.

I can't do this anymore. I'm so tired of running.

Maybe I should just stop and wait for Jane to find me, reach out to her somehow. Maybe I can reason with her, tell her I understand her pain and beg her not to punish me for the harassment I didn't even know was being committed. If she comes clean about what she did to Brett, I will be free.

But then I remember her face the last time I spoke to her,

her eyes like ice. She may have been my friend once, but if she's a murderer, she's gone too far to be reasoned with. And who in their right mind would willingly go to prison when someone else can go in their place?

I finally doze off, but I don't stay asleep for long because I'm woken by the brightness in the room. I open my eyes to see that the curtains are glowing as if it's morning. But it's close to midnight. Drunk with sleep, I get out of bed and go to the window just in time to see the bright headlights of a truck being switched off, then on again. The truck is now reversing fast out of a parking spot directly in front of our room.

As it disappears into the night, the moonlight reveals its color. White.

It moved too fast for me to see the face of the person behind the wheel, but I know there was someone else in the passenger's seat too. Luke's pickup truck looks just like that one.

Is he out of custody already?

And does he know where I am?

CHAPTER 28

At seven in the morning, my phone vibrates next to me, and I flinch, still on edge after seeing the truck last night despite trying to convince myself it was a coincidence. It's Tasha. The phone keeps vibrating, and if I'm not careful, the sound will wake Clark. Surprised she's calling so early, I tiptoe into the bathroom to answer the call.

"Zoe," she says. Her kind voice wraps me in a cocoon. I didn't realize how much I missed being in touch with another adult, someone who cares. I kept hoping Ruth would call to find out how we're doing, maybe ask to speak to Clark, but she never did.

"I'm sorry for calling at this hour, but there's something I think you should know, and I wanted you to hear it from me." She goes quiet and continues in a low voice. "Ruth has passed away, she had a heart attack."

A ball of shock hits my core. "Wh... what?" My mouth is so dry the word comes out distorted. "When did this happen?"

"Yesterday morning she was found by a neighbor. No one knows how long she has been dead."

The idea that Ruth died all alone in her house fills me with a sense of sadness so raw I close my eyes against the pain. When I open them, I'm crying and clutching the phone tight, afraid to let go, wishing I could hug Tasha, longing to go back in time and see Ruth again.

"I feel responsible." Tears are flooding my throat, drowning my words. "It's my fault."

"Why would you say that? She died of a heart attack. No one is responsible for that."

I want to tell her she's wrong, that finding out my secret and Luke being arrested could have pushed her too far. Losing Clark could have been even more painful for her than I imagined.

I lean against the cool tiled wall. "How about—how about Luke?"

"Apparently, he's no longer in custody, but I haven't seen him. I was sad to hear he was bothering you at the cabin." She pauses. "Ruth had no other family members, so I will be arranging her funeral along with some other friends of hers. I was wondering if... Would you like to come?"

What do I tell her? Luke will surely be there, and I can't see him. Even worse, if Jane is really in her hometown, it's possible that she could show up as well.

But Ruth was like family to me and Clark. Will I ever be able to forgive myself if we don't go to her funeral? She did so much for us, and how can I deny Clark the opportunity to say a proper goodbye to the woman who loved him like her own grandson?

"Thank you for letting me know," I whisper finally. "When is the funeral?" I ask.

"A week on Saturday, at the Willow Creek Memorial Cemetery at two p.m. I'm sure Ruth would have wanted to see you there. She really liked you and she was devastated when you left."

It's clear that Ruth did not tell her what she discovered about me, and once again, I'm filled with gratitude toward her.

"And Zoe, it will be really nice to see you again."

I swallow a sob. "It will be nice to see you too."

When I hang up, my hands are shaking, and I sink down onto the toilet seat. My fingertips pressed against my eyes, I remember the woman who was kind to me from the moment I met her, the woman I betrayed by withholding the truth even though she told me the worst things that had ever happened to her.

I can't bear to think I could have contributed to her death, and I hang onto what Tasha said to prevent the guilt from eating me alive. I convince myself that she was probably more devastated about Luke than about us. We were just strangers passing through her life.

I told Tasha that I looked forward to seeing her, but she will not get to see me up close. It will be hard not to be able to speak to her at the funeral. I did everything to push her away, and yet she kept coming back, she never stopped trying to be a good friend to me. But Clark and I won't get close enough for the other mourners to see us. It's safer that way.

I do owe it to Ruth to be there, it's an opportunity to thank her for everything she's done for us, for the protection and love she gave us all those months. I weep for her as if she was my mother and not someone I'd only known for a few months. In my mind, I can see her eyes brightening up whenever Clark ran into her arms. I remember the sound of her voice, so warm and kind before she knew the truth about us. I also remember how weary and broken she sounded the day she asked us to leave. It hurts that her last words to me were drenched in disappointment and pain.

I sneak out of the bathroom and get back into bed. As soon as he feels me beside him, Clark moves closer and curls his little body into mine, but he doesn't wake up.

"I'm sorry," I whisper out loud.

I don't know what I'm sorry for, or who I'm apologizing to. Is it to Ruth? Is it to Clark? Is it to Jane and Denise? And is it too little, too late?

How many more actions will I be forced to take to save me and my son, and what price will I have to pay for them?

CHAPTER 29

Telling Clark that Ruth had died was tough, and in a way, he seemed more upset about her death than Brett's. After hearing the news, he withdrew into himself for a full hour, only speaking when I spoke to him. Finally, he came to me for a hug and asked me if Mrs. Foster is now in heaven with Daddy and I said yes, that they're both watching over us.

This morning, he woke up excited to go to her funeral. I guess it was the idea of going out that brought on the excitement. I don't blame him; being indoors is driving us both crazy.

I hate that we can only say goodbye to Ruth from a distance; I would have liked to throw flowers on her grave.

"Why can't we go to where the people are?" he asks when he notices that we're not getting out of the car. "I want to see Mrs. Foster."

I look at his face for a long time, searching my mind for an answer. "Honey, those people you see over there are Mrs. Foster's family. We were only her friends."

Like I used to do as a kid, I secretly cross the fingers of my left hand. I'm relieved when he gets back to driving the train Tasha gave him across the back of the passenger's seat.

I turn my attention to the group of mourners in the distance, gathered under an oak tree. Given that we're on the opposite side of the street, it's hard to make out any faces, but I can hear people weeping. I watch the casket being lowered into the ground, and I hear the wind blowing through the leaves of the branches hanging above the car before it sweeps across my damp cheek. The smells of cut grass and damp earth drift through the car window.

It's so hard to believe that Ruth is really gone. Wherever she is, I hope she's able to see us down here, to see that we still showed up, and we loved her.

There's a soft tap on the passenger's window.

I turn and meet the eyes of Officer Roland and the first thought in my foggy mind is that I should not have come. I should not have left the motel. What if, like Ruth, he now knows who I am? What if he was waiting for me to show up here?

My lips are parted, but I can't speak. I consider starting the car and just driving off, but that would be even more stupid. He followed me once before and he would probably do it again.

"Who is that policeman, Mommy?" Clark asks from the backseat, and I jump a little at his voice.

Snapped into action, I do what a normal person would do, someone who has nothing to hide. I roll down the window and try to keep my breathing controlled.

"Just someone I know, baby," I say to Clark and turn back to Officer Roland.

He can't see through the dark shades I'm wearing, but my eyes are pleading with him not to do something that would scar my son for life.

Don't arrest me in front of my son, I beg without words.

"I thought that was you," he says, and a shiver of fear vibrates down my spine. "I remember the car."

Of course, he does. He's a police officer, they're trained to recognize these things. They pay attention to detail.

"Good afternoon, Officer." I still can't get myself to call him by his first name.

"Zoe, I'm surprised to see you here. I've been going to Lemon from time to time, and I haven't seen you in a while."

"Yes." I'm trying to be brave, to act normal. He must be wondering why we're sitting here in the car, away from everyone else, and I rack my brain for an explanation. "I don't work there anymore."

"I heard. That's a shame. Why did you stop?"

I shrug. "I wanted something different, that's all. It was a temporary thing."

"Is that your son back there?" He peers through the window to the backseat.

I glance behind me, and notice that Clark has removed his cap. I need to keep talking, to distract Officer Roland from focusing too much on him, and to get a chance to memorize his features.

"Yes, that's my son. How have you been doing?" I ask, changing the subject.

"I've been well, busy chasing criminals." He gives me a bright smile. Maybe he thinks I'm finally interested in him? Maybe that's all this is. "Are you here for Ruth's funeral?" He's saying her name as if he knew her personally, as if he isn't new in town.

"Yes, we are," I say and glance at the mourners again.

"Then why are you not going to join the others?"

"It's... it's too hard. I—"

"I understand." He nods sympathetically. "Did you know her well?"

I shake my head on instinct. "Not that well, but enough."

"Yes, Mommy. We know Mrs. Foster. She was my fairy grandmother."

The officer laughs and peers at Clark through the window again. "Your fairy grandmother, huh? I heard she was a really nice lady."

"Yes." Clark presses his nose against the window, flattening it. "She's in heaven now."

"Well, yes, you're right. She is." He returns to the front window. "This might not be the right time, but would you mind if I ask you a few questions? It might be best if you step out." He glances into the backseat at Clark again.

It's never a good sign when a police officer wants to question someone. And of course, I can't refuse, unless I want him to think I have something to hide.

"Um, sure." I get out of the car.

Out in the open, I run my hands up and down my arms. When I remember that body language says a lot more than words, I drop my arms again. "What is it, Officer? What do you want to know?"

A river of sweat is already making its way down my back. What if this is it? What if this is where it ends? He walks over to my side of the car, gravel crunching beneath his feet. "No need to be nervous. I was just wondering how you're really doing. I heard Luke Foster threatened you at the cabin and I came to check on you a couple of times, but you weren't there. Have you moved out?"

"You're right, we no longer live there." My voice sounds harsher than I want it to be.

He waits for me to say more, and when I don't, he nods. "Is it because of what happened with Luke? Do you know why he was harassing you?"

"I don't... I don't know. Maybe he was jealous that we were staying in his mother's cabin." I tilt up my chin in defiance. "And no, we didn't move out because of him. Some things are just temporary." I clear my throat. "Officer, you're asking an awful lot of questions, but I'm afraid I'm in a hurry. I need to get going."

I discreetly press my palms against the sides of my thighs so my jeans can soak up the sweat. I feel like he's interrogating me. Did Luke say something about me to the cops when he was arrested? If so, why doesn't he just get to the point?

"I apologize for taking up your time. I was just a tad curious, which is not a bad trait for a police officer, some would say." He laughs, but it doesn't reach his eyes, and his intense gaze unnerves me. He's leaning a hand against my car door, as if he's trapping me here on purpose.

From the corner of my eye, I catch movement, then voices make their way to us. The burial is over, and the mourners are all dispersing. Some of them might come in our direction. Luke could be there. Maybe even Jane.

"I'm sorry. I... we really have to go," I croak. "I have to take Clark to—"

"Clark," the officer repeats the name and I give myself an inward kick. "Lovely name for a lovely boy." He continues to stare at me.

More people are walking around us now and my palms and armpits are filling with sweat.

"Have a good day, Officer," I say quickly, taking a step toward the car.

"Sure, you too... Zoe. Talk to you soon," he says, finally moving his hand.

Blood drains from my face. Did I imagine it, or did he hesitate before saying my name?

Before he turns away from me, he cocks his head to one side. "Out of interest, now that you've left the cabin, where are you staying at the moment?"

"In a motel," I say, my words coming out choked. I don't give him the name, but I know that if he wanted to find me for any reason, he would easily be able to. There aren't that many motels nearby. As soon as we get back there, I will pack our things and we will move again, this time much further away.

"Well then, hopefully I'll see you around." He finally walks away.

I'm about to get into my car when I catch sight of Tasha emerging from the crowds. Too late, she sees me and stops walking. Her husband continues to walk on, holding the hands of their two boys. My eyes lock with hers, and her lips curl up into a warm smile as she makes her way toward me.

"Zoe," she says when she gets close enough for me to hear her. Her eyes look swollen from crying, and she's wearing a black cocktail dress, her hair in two braids flat on her scalp.

She wraps me in a hug, but I'm feeling too shaken to respond. My arms remain limp at my sides until finally the desire to connect brings me to put my arms around her as well. I don't know how long we stand there, holding each other, saying so much without words. My glasses are no longer able to prevent my tears from sliding down my cheeks.

Finally, we let go, but Tasha keeps her hands on my shoulders. "Are you okay?"

I nod and dig inside my jeans pocket to pull out a tissue. "I am. I'm okay," I lie.

"I didn't think you would come," she says.

"Neither did I." I remove my glasses and wipe my eyes with the crumpled tissue.

"It's good that you came. The way Ruth spoke about you whenever I saw her, it was clear you and Clark meant a lot to her." Tasha glances in the direction of her husband and kids. "You should join us for the wake we're hosting."

"Thanks, but I'm afraid we can't come." I can't find a reason to give her, so I leave it at that.

"I'm sorry to hear that." Tasha pauses. "If it makes you feel any better, Luke is not here. He didn't show up. He was told about his mother, but he really didn't seem to care."

"Oh, that's terrible."

"I know." She shakes her head ruefully, then looks me up and down. "You've lost a lot of weight, Zoe. Are you sure you're okay? You don't look well."

"I'm just tired." It's an honest answer. I'm tired of running, tired of hiding, tired of hurting. I want to be able to lie in bed and not worry about tomorrow. It feels like I haven't slept for a year, and when I do sleep, the nightmares come to find me.

"I'm sorry, Tasha. I need to take Clark somewhere." I reach for the door handle, yank open the door and get inside. Then I look up at her, a sudden thought coming to me. "By the way, do you happen to know anyone called Jane?"

A cloud passes over her face. "The only Jane I know is the one I went to school with." She shakes her head. "She's no longer in town, though. She was a mess when she left."

Curious to know more, I lean my head out of the window. "Did she know Luke by any chance?"

Tasha rubs her chin, thinking. "I can't say for certain, but since both of them were addicts, I'm sure they would have hung out with the same crowd." She narrows her eyes at me. "Why do you ask?"

I shrug. "I just heard her name mentioned around town and was curious."

"I'm not surprised you've heard about her. She was something, and I don't mean that in a positive way. She damaged her family's reputation so much that her parents left town not long after she did."

"Right... thanks." I start the car, my heart pounding. "I'll keep in touch."

I leave Tasha standing on the sidewalk, a confused expression on her face.

. . .

As soon as we get to the motel, I pack our things and we're back on the road. The only stop we make on our way out of town is to get some groceries. We will be spending another few days indoors.

I don't want to think I could be right. I'm wrestling to keep my thoughts from going to a terrifying place, but that's exactly where I end up. Tasha may not have been certain about Luke and Jane knowing each other, but I am. Just like I now feel confident that Luke found out about me from Jane, and I'm certain they're out to get me. Officer Roland could well be onto me as well, and if he is, he'll be closing in.

Fear stronger than I've ever felt before is coursing through my veins as I drive as far away from Willow Creek as I can. But does it really matter where I go and how fast I run? If they're determined to find me, they will.

We drive until we reach Maple Lane, a town an hour south of Rogersville. I'm too exhausted, both physically and emotionally, to drive any further, so I stop at a roadside motel. A bored-looking man chewing gum with his mouth open checks us in. Behind him, there are only two empty spaces on the rack where the keys hang. It seems only two other rooms are occupied in the entire place. No wonder he looks bored.

In front of the door to our room is a folded newspaper. I pick it up, and as soon as I unfold it, my husband's face stares back at me.

CHAPTER 30

Two days after arriving at the motel, I'm struggling to fall asleep when my phone beeps with a message from Denise's mother.

Turn on the news.
    —Mandy Sanchez

Thankfully, Clark is sleeping like a stone and doesn't even budge when I find the remote in the dark and switch on the TV. The volume is low, and my ears strain to hear every word. I watch the TV screen in disbelief as it bathes the room in color. Cole Wilton's face is on almost all the news channels. Across the top of the screen, in bold type, the headline reads:

Breaking News: The Downfall of Businessman Cole Wilton

Now my mouth is hanging open as I watch the man I used to call my father-in-law being led out of the Black Oyster in handcuffs. He's trying to fight the police off, saying something I can't hear, but the cops have a good handle on him. I'm weak with shock as I watch, and I hold my breath as I try to understand what's going on.

A male reporter with a gelled lock flopping over his forehead throws a glance behind him and then back at the camera. His eyes are shining with excitement, clearly pleased to have landed a viral story.

"Early this morning, hotel mogul Cole Wilton was arrested for the sexual harassment of dozens of his housekeeping staff. You can see him here behind me in handcuffs, being led out of his Fort Haven Black Oyster luxury hotel. We've been told that an anonymous caller tipped off Fort Haven police to a pattern of abuse at the Black Oyster, which kicked off the investigation. Since then, a Facebook account that collected stories of the victims was shared with the local police, and at least ten women, all maids at the hotel, came forward to share their devastating stories of sexual abuse, bribery, and sometimes death threats. We will keep you updated as this explosive story unfolds."

I clutch my hand over my mouth, the bile rising in my throat and a shiver jerking my body. It's like my blood has turned to ice. I never imagined the harassment was that horrific or that Cole was behind it. I'm trying to absorb what's happening but my body and mind are frozen in shock.

How could this happen? Did Brett know what his father was doing?

If so, why didn't he say anything? Why wouldn't he speak up?

Everything I thought I knew is being upended. I clutch the remote, my eyes transfixed on the screen as new and shocking details keep emerging. Several of the maids at the Black Oyster are now being interviewed. I don't know most of them and I imagine they are new, replacing those who left after Cole hurt them. Some of the women are crying, some hugging each other.

"He told me that he only hired me because he wanted to see

if I was a natural redhead," a gorgeous woman says to the camera. "At the time I was grateful because I didn't have any experience for the job. I didn't know I was going to work for a monster."

"Why didn't you tell anyone?" a female reporter asks.

"I was scared. He said he would kill me. And he offered me money. My mother is in a nursing home; I couldn't say no."

Feeling too sick to hear any more, I switch off the TV. As I lie in the dark with my eyes squeezed tight, I think back to the moments I spent in Cole's presence, trying to imagine how I could ever have missed this. When I was around him, I can't remember thinking I was in any danger.

Except for a dream I had, the night Brett and I had our rehearsal dinner. But I can't bear to think about that now.

The next day, Cole's face is all over the papers. In the grocery store, to distract Clark from seeing his grandfather, I give him some money and tell him to move ahead because he's a big boy and can pay for our food. He grins up at me and takes a few steps forward. I'm about to reach for one of the papers when I spot another with a small photo of Cole in a corner of the cover, next to that of a burning building, and I pick it up to read.

Fort Haven's Black Oyster Hotel is burning to the ground. Firefighters surround the place, but the structure that had once boasted power and luxury looks like it's turning to ashes faster than it can be rescued. The place held too many terrible memories, and it's now being destroyed, set on fire by angry protesters. The locals are furious that one of their own has shattered the safe image of Fort Haven. People are going to extremes to demand that something like this never happens again.

If only the memories of what happened in its rooms could be burned too.

*

Back at the motel, the walls are so thin we can hear music being played in the room next door. I find it soothing until I recognize it and my stomach starts to churn.

Let's freeze our memories, baby.

It's our song, the one I was singing along to while cleaning one of the Black Oyster suites with Jane and Denise, the day I first felt a spark with Brett. He walked in and told me, as though I was the only person in the room, that he had always loved that song. We chose it for our wedding dance, and I remember that night like it was yesterday. Brett's arms were so tight around me as he twirled me around the dance floor while his mother watched on with disapproving eyes. I closed my eyes to shut her out, not wanting her to poison my happiness.

In that moment I thought everything would be okay, that we would make it through anything. How wrong I was.

Lying on my back, staring up at the ceiling, I find myself thinking again about the nightmare I had just before the wedding.

Was it really a dream?

CHAPTER 31

SIX YEARS AGO

It's the night before my wedding to Brett, and I'm standing in the entrance to the wedding banquet hall, a little tipsy from the champagne I drank at the rehearsal. Before I leave to go to the apartment I shared with Jane and Denise, who aren't speaking to me and won't come to my big day, I want to see the hall one more time.

Fragrant champagne-colored roses spill from every corner of the room, mingling with the expensive lace and silk. Some of them are also wrapped around the chandelier above the mono-grammed dance floor. Everything is ready for the ceremony tomorrow.

I want to say it's perfect, but is anything ever? More than anything, I would have loved to have Jane and Denise as my bridesmaids, but they turned me down along with their invitation. I would also have wanted my future in-laws to embrace me into their family, but that hasn't happened either, at least not yet. Brett's parents barely smiled during the rehearsal dinner and neither of them said goodnight to me before they left.

But I can't allow myself to get upset, not when Brett and I

are about to start the rest of our lives together. He is all that matters to me. He promised to be my world, and I promised him the same. After three months of dating, I feel like we've known each other all our lives.

I flinch when someone slides their arms around my middle. Then I smell his warm, woodsy cologne before I turned to face him.

"Hello, my wife." He kisses the side of my neck.

"You can't call me that quite yet, Mr. Wilton," I say, leaning in for a kiss. "Just a few more hours left."

"I can't wait." He leans his forehead against mine.

"Are you imagining us dancing here tomorrow?"

"Oh, yes." I smile and hum our wedding song as we sway lightly together.

I allow myself to enjoy our moment alone, then I pull away, my expression serious. "I can't wait to marry you. I just wish we had your parents' blessing."

He kisses me. "Baby, it doesn't matter what my parents think. No one has the right to tell me who to marry. I want you to be my wife and that's all that matters."

"I know, but it would still have been nice if they liked me."

"They will," he says. "With time they will see how amazing you are." He places his hands around the back of my head and kisses me again. "The honeymoon suite is ready for you. You're spending the night here at the hotel."

"I am?" I raise an eyebrow.

"Of course. I wanted it to be a surprise. My girl deserves to sleep in comfort before her wedding day."

It will definitely be nice to sleep in a comfortable suite, where my wedding dress will not be squashed up in a tiny closet.

Brett drives me to my apartment to get my things, before dropping me off at the hotel and asking the staff to help me settle in. We kiss goodnight, and I feel so happy I could fly.

The honeymoon suite is absolutely stunning with a huge king-size bed covered in a silver and white comforter and piles of pillows. It has dark wooden furniture, and long tasseled drapes covering the floor-length windows that overlook the hotel gardens. I look out of the window, where the grounds are lit up by the crescent moon above and the lanterns glowing softly in the distance.

I remove my shoes and step onto the white, plush carpet. I'm not used to luxury like this; it's so soft it feels like I'm walking on a cloud. When my eyes catch the light of the sparkling chandelier above, I hold my breath. It feels like I've fallen into the pages of a book from my childhood.

Before settling into the room, I hang up my wedding dress, then stand in front of it, my gaze misty as I take in the intricate details, following the delicate crystal beads that cascade down the front like an icy waterfall. The silk and satin blend together beautifully, and the dress appears white in the bright light of the chandelier, but on closer inspection the fabric is a delicate cream color.

I can't stop smiling, and I walk over to the white Jacuzzi that sits on the balcony of my suite. It has already been prepared for me, with red rose petals floating on the surface and a bottle of champagne chilling in a bucket of ice on the edge of the tub.

I undress and sink into it, sighing with contentment. Even though I already had several glasses of champagne at the rehearsal dinner, and I know that my body has never been able to handle much alcohol, I pour myself a glass anyway and close my eyes, feeling the sweet, cool liquid prickle its way down my throat.

Before I know it, I've finished my fourth glass, and I force myself to stop. I have never drunk so much before, and doing that the night before my wedding is not smart.

My head spinning, I pull myself out of the tub, but I am unstable on my feet, so I grab onto one of the walls to steady myself. My movements rough and clumsy, I slide on a bathrobe and sway over to the bed.

I close my eyes, and soon drift off into a heavy sleep.

In my dream, someone is knocking on the hotel suite door, and I go to open it to find Cole standing there. He is still wearing the dark-gray suit he had worn at the dinner, but the tie is loose around his neck.

"Hi, Cole," I say in surprise. "What... why are you here?"

"I came to talk." He lets himself into the room, closing the door behind him, then eyeing me with a curious expression. "You're drunk," he says, sounding concerned.

I lean against the wall, trying to steady myself, but I feel sicker with every passing second.

"I want to talk about you marrying my son." He pauses. "Are you sure you're okay?"

I try to speak, but my head is spinning too fast, so I just nod. "Yes. I'm just a little dizzy. I think I need to lie down. Let's talk tomorrow... please." I push away from the wall and take a step, but my knees buckle and I start to sink to the floor.

But before I can reach it, Cole grabs me and holds me up. "Let's get you to bed."

He places an arm underneath my knees and wraps the other around my back, lifting me up. When he lowers me onto the bed, I expect him to leave. But instead, he brings his face close to mine and speaks softly. "Here's your wedding present."

Then to my horror, he lowers his lips to mine.

The next morning, everything is hazy, and I wake up feeling sickened at myself for having such a horrible dream the night before my wedding. I never speak to Brett about it, of course, and everything is perfectly normal between Cole and me. I don't dream of such a terrible thing ever again, and I put it down to too much alcohol combined with my wedding nerves.

It was just a horrible dream.

CHAPTER 32

I stand in the doorway of the small bathroom, my gaze sweeping the room from wall to wall. I can't see him. I can't see Clark.

I left him in the room and now he's gone.

A cold knot of fear clenches inside my belly.

"Clark," I call out, searching the small room as though it were a space with lots of places for a little boy to hide. I drop to my knees and look underneath the bed. Maybe he's playing hide and seek with me?

The only thing under the bed is dusty air.

My son is nowhere to be seen.

It feels as if my heart has stopped beating.

No. This can't be happening.

When I pull myself out of my frozen state, life comes back to my limbs and I run for the door. My heart pounds furiously against my chest, and my throat closes more tightly with each passing second.

I had only been in the bathroom for a few minutes. I was desperate for time alone, time away to cry about what Cole could have done to me.

Normally, whenever I was not in the room with Clark, I secured the door with the chain lock, but it's now dangling free.

I never imagined that he would think of going out on his own, but I shouldn't have been so reckless. He's been bugging me for hours to go outside. He wanted to go to the park. The answer was always "no" and that, of course, frustrated him. He responded with escalating tantrums that were starting to wear both of us out.

I yank open the door and burst outside. I'm in my pajamas and bare feet, but my son is missing and all I care about is finding him.

"Clark?" My voice is shrill, verging on hysterical.

I can't waste any time. I need to find him before he gets far.

Every second feels like an hour as I frantically search around the motel.

A nauseating thought flutters in my stomach. What if Clark did not walk out on his own?

Left with no other choice but to ask for help, I hurry to the reception area. The same man who gave us the keys when we arrived is still there, still looking bored. The place smells of burned coffee and sweat.

He looks up from his newspaper and gives a low grunt. "What do you want?" he asks, as if I'm being a nuisance.

"My son is missing."

He drags a hand through his greasy hair. "And what does that have to do with me? I'm not his babysitter."

"Yes, yes, I know." He's a hateful man, but he's right, and my guilt is heavy in my chest. If I don't find Clark, I'll never forgive myself. "Please help me find him."

"Sorry, I can't help you there." He looks back to his paper. "I'm busy."

"You're reading a newspaper." The anger in my tone takes him by surprise, and he slams the paper down on the desk.

"Lady, your son is not my responsibility. He's probably hiding. Kids do silly things like that, that's why I never wanted any."

Tears of fear and frustration fill my eyes. "Please just help me," I beg. "I searched everywhere."

He raises his eyebrow. "Everywhere?"

He has a point. I haven't searched everywhere—just around the motel and the parking lot. I haven't ventured further into the town, but surely Clark wouldn't be too far from here. I'm sure I was only in the bathroom for a few minutes.

I run back to my room and grab my car keys before driving around the area, hot tears running down my cheeks. This time of evening, there are only a handful of people on the street and none of them is my son.

I should never have left his side when he was so upset, I was so focused on my own problems. Now my worst nightmare has come true. I can't hold back the emotion, and I'm sobbing hard now, brushing tears furiously away from my eyes so I can see the road.

I'm looking for a park somewhere nearby, as I know Clark would have wanted to go there. But I can't find one, and there's no sign of him at all.

If someone finds him before I do, they might alert the cops, and then I might never get Clark back. But at least I'll know he's safe.

I keep stopping to ask passersby if they've seen him, but nobody has seen a little boy walking around on his own. They simply shake their heads and continue with their lives while mine is falling apart.

I drive around in circles for a while, then I head back to the motel. I left the door of our room open just in case, and I'm praying desperately that he will be in there when I get back.

But apart from a taxi parked in the lot, nothing has changed in the area and Clark is still not in our room.

I go around knocking on doors. The only person who opens is a thirty-something-year-old Asian woman, and she doesn't have any good news for me.

"Are you sure he's not in your room?" the woman asks when I start crying again.

"No, he's not." I choke. "I can't find him."

"Has he done anything like this before? I mean... run off on his own?"

"No." I shake my head. "Never."

"Then you have to call the police," the woman says. "They will find him."

"I will," I say. I know I'll be arrested as soon as the cops realize who I am. But right now the only thing that matters is making sure Clark is okay.

The woman is kind enough to help me look around the perimeter of the motel again with no success, and she apologizes for not being able to help me before returning to her room.

The sun is starting to set, the sky bruised purple and red, and Clark is still out there, all alone.

I return to my room to get my phone, but it's not on the bedside table where I left it.

My body stiffens in horror.

I run back to reception to ask if I can use the phone, but that infuriating man is no longer behind the reception desk. I'm about to leave when he walks in from outside, eating a burger. Ketchup is dripping onto his chin and clinging to his beard.

"You again," he says, chewing. He raises the burger to his mouth again, a Rolex glinting in the light.

"Look, I need to call the police right away. Please can I use your phone? I can't find mine."

He shakes his head. "It's not working."

I can tell he's lying. He doesn't want to help me and I don't understand why. A child is missing, and he doesn't seem to care at all.

"Please, I'm begging you. My son is still missing. I need to call the police. Someone took him." My voice is getting louder and louder as he chews away, and I want to grab the burger from his hands and smash it into his face. But I need his help.

"Ma'am, as I said, my phone is not working." He pushes the nail of his pinkie between his two front teeth to remove whatever is stuck there, and he continues to eat noisily as he disappears through a door behind the reception desk.

I scan the surface for the phone, but I can't see it.

Swearing, I rush out of the door. I'll just ask the first person I see if I can use their phone. My skin is hot, my hands clammy, and my thighs are aching from running.

The parking lot is quiet except for a car pulling out, and it's the woman who had helped me look for Clark. I try to run after her car, but it has already turned into the main road.

Running back into the hotel, I notice that the room next to ours has its light on, and I slam my fists against it. Sweat is pouring into my eyes, mixing with my tears.

"Come in," a man calls from the other side, and I push down the door handle.

When the door swings open, I reel back in shock.

"Mommy." Clark looks up and our eyes meet. "Look, Grandpa came to visit us."

Clark is on the couch, sitting next to Cole.

Cole, the monster who hurt so many people.

Including me, I realize in a horrific jolt that forces its way through my body.

"Surprised to see me?" He raises an eyebrow, his face twisting into a sneer.

CHAPTER 33

He shouldn't be here. He should be behind bars or in police custody, but he's sitting right there in front of me with a broad smile plastered on his face, wearing one of his designer suits. You'd think he's about to attend a meeting.

"Let him go." I choke out the words, and my body shakes so much my teeth are chattering. I have never been more terrified of anyone in my life or so overcome with the kind of hate that rips you apart.

I've gone through that night at the hotel over and over in my mind and I'm more convinced than ever that he really did assault me, that it wasn't a dream. Until now, I always thought Cole to be an okay father-in-law. Even if he wasn't fully on board with me marrying his son, he didn't give me a hard time about it, not like Nora. And all along I thought she was the one who was trying to ruin my marriage, who had poisoned Brett's life. Now I wonder if she acted that way because she knew, or at least suspected, what Cole was up to. Perhaps she tried to control Brett because she felt so powerless.

I should never have dismissed what happened the night before my wedding as a dream. I think it was my mind's way of protecting me from the trauma, unable to accept what had happened.

Cole tightens his arms around Clark and my eyes grow hot with rage. I take in the pale watch-shaped mark circling his wrist, and hazily I realize that the motel receptionist wouldn't help me because Cole got to him first. He paid him with his own Rolex.

"After all this time, no hello?" he asks, drawing out his words. "I'm quite disappointed, Meghan. Or is it Zoe now?"

"Let go of my son." I ball my hands into fists. "Clark, baby, come to Mommy." I unfurl my fingers and stretch out my arms for him to run into.

Clark shakes his head and leans into Cole. "I want to stay with Grandpa. We had fun. Grandpa bought me ice cream. We left you some in the fridge, Mommy."

There really is a mini fridge in this room, and I also notice that Clark is playing with an expensive-looking black and gold toy plane. My skin feels ice-cold. When I thought we were safe hiding in our motel room, was Cole right next door with only a wall between us?

Was he the person who played my wedding song?

How did he know we were here?

Cole raises one of his hands and runs it over my son's hair. "I missed you, my boy," he says to Clark.

"Cole, please, don't do this." I'm seething with rage, but I must control my temper for Clark's sake. I don't know this man at all, not anymore. But I know he is dangerous, perverted, devoid of compassion, and I can't bear to think about what he could be capable of.

His gaze still on me, Cole gets to his feet and reaches into his pocket for a phone... my phone. He hands it to Clark. "Go and play a game in the bathroom. Your mommy and I need to speak about something important." He ruffles his hair. "Go on, boy. Don't come out until I tell you to, then soon I'll let you fly on a real airplane."

"Really? Yay!" Clark's eyes light up as he beams up at Cole. Then he does as he's told.

An airplane? A horrible realization sinks into me. Cole is here to take Clark away. He must be on the run himself, and he's going to escape the country with my son. As soon as the bathroom door closes, I rush to it and plant myself in front. I will do anything to protect Clark. Cole will have to go through me, and I will fight with every ounce of strength I have.

"What do you want from me?" I whisper furiously. "Why don't you leave us alone?"

Cole strokes his stubble. "You know exactly what I want from you, black widow."

"I didn't." I lower my voice. "I didn't kill Brett."

Cole laughs darkly, then lowers himself into the couch again. He's so relaxed, as if he's in no hurry at all. "That's the story you've been telling yourself all these months?"

"It's the truth. But you, you're pure evil. You... all those things... I know what you did to all those women, you disgusting pig. You did to them what you did to me."

"Oh, I thought you forgot about that night?" he says lightly, narrowing his eyes. "You had drunk so much alcohol, you silly little girl. If you remembered, why didn't you tell Brett that I owned you before he did?"

Owned me. I feel sick. I don't remember anything clearly beyond the kiss, it's all a blur.

I clench my fists. I want to lunge for him, to claw out his eyes, but I know I won't win. I need to be smart, for Clark.

"Please, Cole. Leave us in peace. I won't... I won't tell anyone you were here." As I say the words, it occurs to me that I wouldn't be surprised if the police actually let him go. Even with the overwhelming evidence stacked up against him, he won't be the first powerful man to evade justice.

"You really think it's that simple?" He shakes his head, plants his hands on his thighs and pushes to his full intimidating height. "I've been waiting for this moment for so long, to face the woman who killed my son, to make sure you get what you deserve." He shoves his hands into his pockets. "For a while there, it seemed you had disappeared from the face of the Earth. I thought of letting you be, allowing you to spend the rest of your life looking over your shoulder. But I changed my mind. You killed my boy, and you took Ashton away from me. I won't allow you to keep him from me, Meghan." He chuckles. "It was quite entertaining getting calls from so many people who claimed to have seen you. They all wanted the twenty thousand dollars, and as I had expected, most of them ignored the cops and came straight to me asking for a higher reward. Many were liars, of course, except one honest man, who told me that he saw you at a funeral. He helped me track down where you were staying. He really worked for his money."

"Who?" The word comes out like a bullet.

Cole runs a hand through his thick hair. "Oh, some local cop."

I gape at him, speechless. Roland is a crooked cop? Luke must have told him who I was when he was arrested, just as I feared, and he was at the funeral waiting for me to show up. When I left Ruth's funeral, he must have followed me here.

And here I was thinking he was interested in me.

"I don't blame him for coming to me," continues Cole casually. "Some police officers are not paid enough."

"What do you want from me?" I ask through clenched teeth. "Why are you here?"

Behind me, a tiny voice makes itself heard through the thin door. "Can I come out now?" Clark calls.

"Not yet, my boy." Cole smiles at me. "Very soon."

"Okay," Clark squeals with delight. "Then we can go flying?"

"Yes, we'll go on a fun adventure. First of all, we will go fishing and I'll teach you to hunt at my cabin." His eyes are still fixed on mine. "You remember the cabin, don't you, Meghan?"

I do know what he's talking about, although I don't know why he cares. Once or twice a month, he and Brett went hunting there, in a small village near Fort Haven. Brett hated going, but for reasons I never understood, he never said no. And when Clark was two, he took us with him. When Cole saw that Brett had brought the two of us along, they ended up arguing. It was one of the few times I heard Cole lose his temper and I couldn't understand why he didn't want us there. I guess he just wanted to spend alone time with his son. After Cole left in a rage, we ended up spending the weekend at the cabin, just the three of us. We fished, we went for walks in the small town, and bought fresh fruits and vegetables from the locals.

It makes me feel ill now to think that all that time while I was friendly with Cole, hanging out with him and trying to prove I was a good wife to his son, he knew exactly what he'd done to me.

Cole takes a step forward, and I jump. "By the way, Meghan, I know it was you. You messed with my business. You called people and told them damaging things about me."

"I did not. But you deserve to go to prison for what you did." I swallow hard and lower my voice. "You are a rapist."

"Those women were whores. They offered themselves willingly to me, just like you. I didn't commit any crimes, and the cops have nothing on me."

"Denise wasn't a prostitute. You sexually assaulted her, and me. That is a crime." My voice is soft so Clark can't hear, but the hatred I feel for Cole is loud and clear.

"Ah, Denise Sanchez, I remember her." He sighs, shoves his hands into his pockets, and turns to the window.

"You drove her to suicide, Cole." I blink back tears. "What you did killed her."

"She was too much trouble," he growls without turning to look at me.

Like a flash of lightning, it comes to me. Denise's mother didn't want to believe her daughter would take her own life. Now I think maybe she was right.

She was probably hellbent on exposing Cole. I don't want to believe that my father-in-law is a murderer, but he has shown himself to be capable of more than I could ever imagine. Who wouldn't kill to keep such hideous crimes hidden?

Bile rising in my throat, my mind turns to Brett. Exactly how much did he know about what his father was up to?

Did he know, and decided he wanted to come clean before he died?

Is that what he told Cole earlier that day?

As the thought spreads through me like wildfire, my breath comes in short and sharp gasps, and I have to will myself not to descend into panic. I need to take my son and get away from Cole before I become his next victim.

Adrenaline floods back into my body and I slowly rise to my feet.

His back is still turned to me, and I twist the bathroom handle and yank open the door. I grab Clark's arm and pull him out.

"Ouch, Mommy," he complains, and Cole whips back to face me with eyes like thunder.

"What do you think you're doing? Don't make another stupid mistake, Meghan."

Ignoring him, I push Clark toward the front door, standing between him and Cole. "Go to the car, Clark. It's open."

"But, Mom, Grandpa—"

"I said go. Now. Run." My voice is firmer than he has ever

heard it, so he opens the door and runs out, still holding my phone.

When Cole takes a step toward me, I grab a standing lamp from nearby and raise it above my head. "Don't you dare come near me or my son ever again."

"You don't get it, do you?" Cole laughs. "You can't go anywhere that I won't find you." He comes even closer. "You have no idea what I'm capable of."

I don't waste time; I swing the lamp as hard as I can. It collides with his body, and he loses his balance and topples into the TV. He sends it crashing to the floor, with him following right after it.

I'm about to run out of the room when he starts laughing again. "Go ahead and walk out that door. See how far you'll get."

"Go to hell." I run out of the room.

"I won't let you take my son from me," he shouts. His words slam against my heart, and I almost stumble with shock, but I keep moving until I'm behind the wheel.

The moment I start the car, he appears in the doorway and runs, still fast despite his limp, to the taxi I saw in the parking lot earlier.

CHAPTER 34

Cole raped me that night.

After realizing it wasn't a nightmare but a real memory I have suppressed all this time, I suspected that it went that far. But I didn't want to believe it. The flashing images I have from that night are so unclear. Perhaps my mind still refuses to show me what happened. I wanted so much to believe it stopped at a kiss, but he has just confessed. And now I don't even know how to feel, how to think. My mind and body are in complete disarray.

"You're driving too fast, Mommy," Clark says for the fourth time.

I peer into the rearview mirror and tension melts from my shoulders.

Not a single car is behind us. We lost him.

Cole's taxi was behind us for at least half an hour, not even speeding, just torturing me.

"I'm sorry, baby." I take a quick glance at Clark and I shudder inwardly.

He *does* resemble Cole. I'd never noticed how much. He

has the same squinting, slate-gray eyes and slightly upturned nose.

No, I think, disgust welling up inside me. Clark is Brett's son, not his father's. It's no surprise that he resembles Cole. It wouldn't be the first time a child resembles its grandparent.

But the cramps of fear in my belly refuse to let up, and the nagging little voice inside my head asks, "What if?"

"Mommy, why are you angry with Grandpa?"

What do I tell Clark? I can't possibly allow him to continue thinking Cole is a saint.

"I'm sorry, baby, but your grandfather is not a good person. Promise me that you will not go anywhere with him again. He did some bad things."

"What did he do? Did he hurt you?"

You have no idea. You have no idea how much he hurt me. What he did to me I cannot put into words.

That's what I want to tell him, but I can't. That part of the truth he cannot know, at least not yet. I don't want to shatter his innocence completely. But eventually, I might not have a choice. Cole's crimes have become a national story. Clark is bound to see him on the news sometime.

"He wants to hurt us," I say. I don't want to scare Clark, but I need him to know he isn't safe with Cole. It's the truth. He wants to destroy us. He wants to take my son away from me and send me to prison for a crime someone else committed.

My insides shudder when I return to the possibility that Cole could have killed his own son, that maybe Brett threatened to expose him, having nothing to lose since he believed that the cancer would soon kill him. There are many people who choose to make things right when they're close to death's door, to clear their conscience. Perhaps Brett told Cole of his plan to end his life, and Cole decided to make sure it happened before he could tell anyone what he knew. I don't know how he would have managed it that night, but right now I would believe Cole is capable of anything.

"But Grandpa's nice," Clark says. "I miss him."

"No, he's not, Clark. He's not a nice person," I say between clenched teeth. "I need you to understand that. I need you to trust Mommy right now."

"Is that why he and Grandma didn't visit us in the cabin? Is she a bad person too?"

"Yes, they both are." I tighten my hands around the steering wheel, speeding up. "We can't let them come near us again."

If Nora covered up her husband's crimes, then she, too, is a terrible person, and I would never trust her with my son.

A red Honda has appeared behind us, its headlights blinking on and off. A warning? My fear starts pushing me to the edge of my sanity again, but then the car turns into another road. I wipe my forehead with the back of my hand and release the breath I've been holding.

How long until he shows up again? What if he's ahead of us, waiting? But he doesn't know where we are headed. Neither do I, in fact. My plan so far has simply been to get as far away from him as possible.

It's only a few minutes later that I notice we are about twenty minutes from Willow Creek. It feels like I'm going home. I did feel safe there for a while, and that's the only place in the world where I have a friend who wants to help. Of course, there's a risk I'll see Officer Roland, but I don't know where else to go.

I really do need a friend right now. And now that I don't think Jane is a murderer, I'm not afraid of her or even Luke. Not anymore. They may have tormented me, but I doubt they planned to do me any actual harm.

I'm afraid that Cole might hurt Tasha if she helps me, but I need her. She did promise that she will be there for me, and I don't know where else to turn.

I pull over and dial her number, but when she picks up, I'm unable to speak clearly because my throat is closing up with emotion.

"Zoe," she says. "Honey, is that you?"

"I need your help, Tasha," I blurt out. "Please, I don't know what to do. I don't know where to go."

I should probably go to the police, but how can I trust them to keep me and Clark safe? They let Cole go, and Officer Roland put him onto me even though he must have known I would be in danger.

My head hurts too much to think about what to do next. I need someone else to think for me, to tell me what to do.

"Where are you?" Tasha asks, her voice high-pitched with worry. "Are you okay?"

"No." My voice is smothered by tears. "I'm not okay. I'm on my way into town. I'm in danger, I think."

"Come to our house, right now. Whatever is going on, just come here, okay?"

"I can't." I want to. I want to find a safe place to hide, but I could be leading Cole straight to the people who are trying to help me. I don't want anyone to get hurt because of me. "He's after me. If I come to you, you will probably be in danger, too."

I feel foolish. What was the point of calling Tasha if I'm refusing her help?

"Who is after you?" she asks.

"My... my father-in-law. He's dangerous." I glance at Clark, who is on the verge of falling asleep. "I can't say more now."

Tasha is quiet for a few moments before she speaks. "Tell me where you are. I'll come to you. Then you can tell me everything."

"I'm headed to Willow Creek," I say.

"Perfect. Let's meet at a crowded place somewhere."

"Where?" I don't know what place in Willow Creek would be crowded late at night.

"Come to my brother's club, the Night Owl. Ask for Samuel, and I'll meet you there. How far away are you?"

"Not far. We should arrive in about fifteen or so minutes."

"Good. I'm on my way."

CHAPTER 35

People are spilling in and out of the Night Owl, and I slow down first, observing the place, making sure that Cole is not among the people gathered outside the entrance. He couldn't possibly know I'm here, but I'm still paranoid. I ease my anxiety with the thought that he won't be able to do anything to me without someone stepping up to help.

Instead of parking close to the club, I find a spot a few blocks away, close to a hotel. If he's following me, there's a chance Cole will think I'm inside the hotel instead of the night club.

When Clark opens his eyes, he's disoriented for a moment, and I feel terrible for waking him.

"Where are we?" he asks, looking out the window.

"We're going to see Tasha. Would you like that? We miss her, don't we?"

He brightens up a little, but only nods. Exhaustion is written all over his face. I dream of a day when he can rest without interruption.

"Sweetheart, listen to Mommy very carefully." I reach for

his hand. "I need you to be a good boy, okay? If you see Grandpa, don't go to him. Remember what I said to you?"

He nods. "He's not a nice man. He wants to hurt us."

I can tell he wants to ask more questions but doesn't know the right ones or how to phrase them.

"Are we going to Lemon?" he asks.

"No, we're not." I help him out of his car seat. "Tasha wants us to meet at another place."

"What will Grandpa do if he finds us?"

"He won't," I say with determination.

Clark doesn't ask any more questions. In silence, I pull his baseball cap over his head and we hurry hand in hand down the street. I glance over my shoulder every few seconds and peer into the windows of every car that passes.

Just because I don't see him doesn't mean he's not nearby.

We make it to the club without anything happening, and the clubbers milling around the entrance glance at me as they puff their cigarettes. It's obvious they're judging me. What kind of mother would bring a child to a club when he should be in bed fast asleep?

The bouncer is a boulder of a man with half his head shaved and the other adorned by spiky hair. He's wearing a tight T-shirt, with the word "Bouncer" across the front. The way he's towering over me reminds me of Cole. They're both intimidating, but in different ways.

"Invitation only tonight." He throws Clark a look. "And no kids allowed."

I pull Clark closer to me. His little body is trembling as he buries his face into my side.

"We were invited here," I say.

Mr. Bouncer folds his arms across his chest. "Your name?"

"Megh... Zoe, I'm Zoe." Now that the past has caught up with me, it's becoming harder to think of myself as Zoe. "Samuel is my friend's brother. She told us to come here."

The bouncer's face relaxes, and he places a hand on top of Clark's head. "I was just making sure. Samuel is expecting you, go up to the bar." He steps aside and we make our way through the throng of people.

Clark is holding my hand and covering his ear at the same time. The music is so loud, I feel my body vibrate. I can't even imagine how it must be for him.

The bartender leans across the counter, his tattooed arms folded on the surface. "What can I get you?" he shouts over the noise.

"Nothing, thank you. Samuel is expecting us."

"I'll get him." He looks down at Clark, who has just hopped up onto a high stool. "Sorry, he needs to get down from there. It's the law." The man disappears, and a woman with a straight ponytail immediately replaces him behind the bar as Clark hops back down again.

She fills a glass with orange juice and a straw and hands it to me. "For the little guy." She nods toward Clark. "On the house." She winks at me, and I thank her.

Clark drinks the juice gratefully. He must be hungry as well; I'll have to find a way to get him something to eat. Looking around me, I'm glad that most of the guests are dressed appropriately. Only a few people are dancing. The rest are at the bar or sitting on red leather couches on one side of the dance floor.

Samuel, a man with short dreadlocks and dressed in a suit, finally comes to meet us, and like Tasha, he seems to be very friendly. "I'm sorry you had to wait so long." He shakes my hand. "Come with me. Let's get the boy out of this loud place."

As we follow him down a carpeted corridor with black and white rock and roll posters on the wall, I'm grateful he's not wasting time by asking questions.

"Where are we going?" I ask, suddenly uneasy.

"I was told to keep you safe, so that's what I'm doing." He leads us down a flight of stairs to a wine cellar.

The stairwell is spooky with its dim lighting and an eerie echo, and Clark must feel it too because he grips my hand even tighter.

As soon as the heavy door at the bottom of the stairs shuts, the noise from the club above dies. It's so quiet in the basement that I can hear my own heart thudding.

"Tasha said you needed a safe place. This is it, make yourselves at home. She said she'd be here in about ten minutes."

It's a large wine cellar that also serves as an office and a living room. A wooden desk is piled high with papers and folders, and a large, black couch is pushed against one wall, its paint chipped and peeling, making it look almost like an animal print. A red velvet couch stands next to it with a tall lamp on its right side. A strong smell of damp walls and sandalwood cologne permeates the space, and the flickering lighting pulses painfully through my brain.

Samuel calls for someone to bring us more drinks and a cheeseburger for Clark, and we sit down on battered leather chairs opposite some dusty wine racks as we wait for them to arrive.

"Thank you." I'm so moved by the help I'm getting from a stranger.

"That's all right. Tasha mentioned you're in danger."

"Um... yeah. We—"

"You don't have to explain. All I'm going to say is that you picked the right person to help you out. She said you're a good friend of hers."

Heat spreads through my chest. "Yes, yes, I am."

"Well, anyone who is Tasha's friend is my friend. So, whatever help you need, I'm here. I'm going upstairs for a while to see if she's arrived. You stay here and don't come up under any circumstances. The key is in the lock. Lock the door if it makes you feel safer."

As soon as the burger and drinks arrive and he leaves, that's exactly what I do. Then I sit down and watch Clark eating his burger like he hasn't eaten in days.

Shortly after Samuel leaves, someone knocks on the door. I'm afraid to open it, but Tasha calls my name from the other side. The first thing she does when I open the door is gather me into her arms. "Thank God you're okay." She pulls me closer.

I hold on to her as if for dear life. "Thank you so much for everything, Tasha."

I only hope she won't regret helping me after she discovers who I really am, and who I'm running from.

From over her shoulder, Samuel gives me a nod and returns to his guests, leaving us alone to talk. It's time for the truth to come out. If Tasha is going to help me, I need to be honest with her about everything.

I start from the very beginning. I tell her how Cole raped me, how I married his son, how Brett was diagnosed with cancer and begged me to end his life, and everything that happened after. Tasha is already familiar with the story from the news, so I don't have to fill in all the details. What she also knows is that Cole was indeed released from custody. Many women who came forward have since retracted their stories and there's no longer sufficient evidence to prove he committed the crimes he's charged with.

"Please tell me you didn't really kill your husband," she says after a long silence, moving closer so Clark won't hear us.

He's wearing headphones and watching cartoons on Tasha's phone while lying on a couch in a corner.

I shake my head. "No, I didn't, I swear. I almost... but I couldn't." I shut my eyes. "He died anyway. I thought he killed himself, but not anymore. I think his father did it. And I don't think he's the only person he killed. I think he also killed one of the women he raped, and she was my friend."

"Oh, my God." She covers her mouth, her eyes wide. "The girl who committed suicide? You think it was murder?"

I nod. "I think my friend and Brett planned to expose him, so he got rid of them. Tasha, I'm so sorry I didn't tell you who I am... who I was."

She takes hold of my hands and sighs. "Zoe, I already knew who you were. Ruth told me not long before she died."

"And you still want to help me?"

"I do, because I don't believe you did it. I haven't known you for long, but my gut tells me you're not a murderer."

"Thank you. I'm so grateful, that means everything to me," I say, choking back a sob. "I'm so scared," I continue after a moment. "I'm scared for me and for Clark. If Cole finds us again, he could kill me and take him. I can't let a man like him raise my son."

"We won't let that monster come near Clark ever again. I promise I'll do whatever I can to help you, but I honestly think you should go straight to the police. Tell them everything you found out. They might believe you." She squeezes my hand. "I believe you."

"But Cole has connections. That police officer that you thought was interested in me; he's the one who told him where I was. I don't know if I can trust any cops right now."

Tasha's mouth falls open. "You're kidding."

"No. Cole told me himself that he called him for the reward. I guess he was a decent policeman until he saw the reward on my head and called Cole."

"It makes sense now. That man has not been seen since the day he showed up at Ruth's funeral. He used to come to the restaurant almost every day, and then he stopped. Who knows? Maybe he was fired, or he left to spend his dirty money elsewhere."

"He's gone? Thank God."

"I think so. But your father-in-law could be anywhere. He needs to go to prison for his crimes, and you need to stop running." She pulls me into another hug. "I wish you had told me sooner. You didn't have to go through all that alone." She leans back and puts her hands on my shoulders. "I know it's terrifying, but that man can't just get away with murder and rape. You have the power to make sure that doesn't happen. You are a survivor and your story could be just what the cops need to throw him into prison. I'll be here for you every step of the way."

"But is my story enough? They've already thrown out so many other women's testimonies. I know you're right, he needs to be in prison, but..." I pause, my mind racing. "I think I know what to do. I have an inkling about where I could find some evidence, maybe."

"Do what you have to do and I will take care of Clark. We'll take him and the boys somewhere safe."

"Thank you." We hold each other for a long time until I pull away. "I'll do it. I'll make sure Cole doesn't get away with it."

CHAPTER 36

After spending the night in a small room above the Night Owl, I find the courage to call the Willow Creek Police Department. When I reveal who I am, I'm promptly transferred to a man named Dan Mason, the lead detective. I guess only he is qualified to deal with such a high-profile case. He asks me to come in, but I refuse because there's no guarantee they won't arrest me.

"I'm calling to tell you that my father-in-law is not only guilty of raping those women, but he also murdered one of the women he raped: my friend Denise Sanchez. And I will find the proof."

I'll only show my face to the police when I have the evidence that will help them arrest Cole and exonerate me. If the police were not able to find anything at the hotel before it burned down, or at Cole and Nora's house, there's one other place they have not checked, and given the corruption in law enforcement that I've now experienced myself, I'm not going to tell them before I have the evidence safely in my hands. It's a place they may not even know exists. Cole's cabin, the place that Brett used to call his father's man cave. Whatever evidence

I'm looking for might be there. I don't know what it could be: pictures? A diary? But I just have to hope there is something.

After calling the cops, I spend the next hours napping with Clark or playing video games with him, and when Samuel occupies him, I check the news while counting down the hours.

The clock has just struck 6 p.m. when I hop onto the only daily bus headed for Rustdale, the village town where Cole's cabin is located. To get there, though, I'll have to pass through Fort Haven.

Four hours later, the bus drives through the town I thought I'd never see again. The lights are warm and inviting, but I will never feel at home there again.

I feel uneasy leaving Clark behind, but Tasha convinced me that it's safer this way, and I agreed. This is something I need to do alone, and I trust Tasha. She promised me she would take great care of my son.

I'm pretty sure Cole's main priority is coming after me first, and that means Clark is safe from him for now.

Around 10 p.m. the bus stutters to a halt in Rustdale. It's a struggle to get to my feet as my knees are so weak with nerves, but I force myself not to give up.

My hair is styled differently and I'm wearing clothes that Tasha's brother gave me, that once belonged to an ex-girlfriend of his. Leather pants with a jean jacket and a matching cap are not something I would normally wear, but that suits me well enough. I'm someone else now. I have been broken, crushed. There's barely anything of the old me left behind. The only part that remains alive is the angry, determined flame that burns inside me, fueled by love for my son, willing to fight tooth and nail to keep him safe and to get our lives back for his sake. Everything else has been destroyed by Cole.

"Ma'am, are you getting off?" a pregnant woman asks from behind me.

"Sorry," I murmur when I realize I'm blocking the way, then I get off the bus.

When it drives off, I halt, suddenly afraid. What if I find nothing to prove Cole is a rapist and a murderer? What will I do then?

As I wander around the bus stop, I think again about the possibility that Clark could be Cole's son and the urge to vomit hits me so hard that I throw up into a nearby bush. A woman walking by curses under her breath and distances herself from me, but I'm too far gone to care what anyone thinks of me being sick in a public place.

The dark street is now deserted with only the occasional person walking by. I had planned on staying at a hotel first and going to the cabin in the morning, but I can't wait any longer. I straighten up, push my shoulders back, and wipe my mouth with a napkin from my handbag. I might feel weak inside, but nothing will stop me from seeking justice.

I need Cole to go to prison. He has to hurt, to experience how it feels to be stripped of everything you know, everything you cherish.

The Brittle Rose cabin is in the woods, at least twenty minutes from the bus stop, so I take a taxi. During the drive, the taxi driver plays a few gospel songs on the radio, and I wish they could soothe me, but only Cole's arrest would do that. Still, I close my eyes and allow the music to wash over me.

"Sir, would you mind waiting for me?" I ask when we arrive. I don't want to be out here all alone.

I gaze out of the window into the darkness. Everything is pitch black. I don't know if the spare key is still where it used to be, but I'll find a way to get inside in any case, breaking the windows if I have to.

"No problem." The man reaches for his headphones on the passenger's seat. "Take all the time you need. But it will cost extra."

"That's fine," I say.

Outside, the air is comfortably warm against my skin and it smells of damp earth and pine. I remember loving the scents on the air that time I came here with Brett. But this time, it just makes me feel nauseous again. I make my way to the front door, glancing back to make sure the taxi is still waiting. To my surprise, the key is still in its usual place underneath a potted plant on the porch.

In contrast to outside, the air inside is heavy and tainted. Something is not right, and I feel it. I switch on the light, and it floods the luxurious cabin. The leather couch, massage chair, and expensive throw pillows and rugs make it a perfect bachelor escape. Some might find the place relaxing, but not me, not anymore. Standing inside it, I get a bitter tang in my mouth and an impulse to flee.

A chilly silence surrounds the place, daring me to disturb it. I'm dreading what it hides from the world, what secrets it's harboring. I suddenly feel ill-equipped to do this, but it's too late to turn back and I refuse to leave empty-handed.

There's no time to waste. This might be my only chance to make things right for everyone who suffered at the hands of Cole Wilton, and to protect the future of my son.

White-hot anger is flooding through my veins, giving me the courage I need.

I want to be Cole's greatest mistake ever. I want him to regret the day he laid a hand on me.

CHAPTER 37

The cabin has two bedrooms in total, but only one seems functional. The other is empty from floor to ceiling; aside from the paneled walls and dark floorboards, there's nothing inside. I rub my arms to erase the goosebumps on my skin. Even the air is devoid of warmth. When I was at the cabin with Clark, we slept with Brett in the room that's now empty. Why has it been cleared?

I step out of the room and head to the other bedroom, which has the same feel to it as a suite at the Black Oyster. As I stand in the doorway, my gaze taking in the vintage leather couch by the window that overlooks a lake, and the king-sized bed, it's hard for me to breathe. I can't help but think back to that night, to the dream I now know was reality.

I brace myself and step farther into the room. Searching it doesn't take long, again there's nothing to find. The only thing in the closet is an empty designer suitcase. The drawers have been cleared out and the bathroom cabinets are bare.

I search the rest of the cabin and come across a cupboard in the living room with three rifles propped up inside it. I step back, a churning feeling in my stomach, and shut it again. Guns make me nervous.

Suddenly, I hear something slamming, and I rush to the window in a panic, but I'm relieved to see only the taxi driver smoking a cigarette outside his car. He must have been shutting the car door. I drop the curtain, give myself a shake and turn back to the room.

Maybe this was a mistake. I came all this way without a clear plan of exactly what I was looking for, and there might not be anything here anyway. It looks like Cole has recently cleared the place out. The best thing for me to do is probably to leave, but my hunger for revenge has me in a vice and refuses to let go.

I keep thinking that if I'm surrounded by Cole's possessions, I might find something, anything. There are people like him who like to keep souvenirs of their victims. A man as sick as Cole could do the same. And this is his personal space, the place he comes to relax. Maybe it's also the place he comes to when he wants to reminisce about his crimes, far away from his wife and his respectable life. He used to come here with Brett once or twice a month, but he also comes on his own at least once a week.

I will myself to be strong, thinking about how, after all this is over, Clark and I can rebuild our lives properly and how happy he will be. The mere thought of running again exhausts me. Clark is the reason I search the cabin again. I want to be free to raise my son without fear.

My and Brett's son. Not Cole's.

I search every room again, including the kitchen where I find an unfinished mug of coffee on the counter, which makes me suspect that Cole was at the cabin recently. I need to search faster and get the hell out.

I don't care that I'm moving things out of their usual places. Maybe a part of me wants him to know I was here. My search leads to nothing, and I soon realize the harsh smell in the air is disinfectant. Someone has been here, scrubbing the place clean.

I return to the empty room again, standing in the middle, turning from one side to the other, wondering if there's something I'm missing, something I can't see. I've searched every nook, and yet I feel as if there's something else hiding in the shadows. I don't want to give up yet.

But there's nothing here. It was foolish of me to think Cole would be so careless to leave evidence lying around in plain sight. I need to get out of the place, to head to the only hotel in town, and get some sleep. My head will be clearer in the morning, and I will be able to make better decisions. I might have to get the cops involved and just hope they are trustworthy. If I notify them of the cabin's existence and location, they might be able to find something. But I won't be here when they arrive. I won't let them come near me until Cole is the prime murder suspect.

Biting hard on my lower lip, I slump against one of the walls, drop my handbag to the floor and slide down next to it. I draw my knees to my body and hug them, resting my forehead against them. After sitting on the floor for a while, too weak to get up, I remember that the taxi driver is waiting for me outside. Maybe it's time to give up.

As I shift my weight, struggling to get to my feet, the floor creaks underneath me and an idea hits me. On my hands and knees, I crawl around the area. Then I spring to my feet and start hopping at random places. Only a quarter of the room has creaking floorboards.

My heart is pounding in my ears when I crouch down again and feel the floor for more clues, slamming my fists into it. One of my nails snaps close to the nail bed when I insert it between two slabs of wood. It hurts, but I don't stop. In comparison to my burning desire to find something useful, the pain is nothing. But I grab a knife from the kitchen and try again. Finally, a board is loosened enough to reveal something that is hidden inside.

My instinct was right. I'm staring at the top of a brown box that has been taped shut.

I get to work removing more of the floorboards to get full access to the box. There's more than one; I'm seeing at least three, all of them taped shut.

Sweat is dripping from my forehead as I cut through the tape and start opening the first box without lifting it from its hiding place. It's full of DVDs in white cases, at least a dozen of them. The spines of the cases are labeled with numbers.

102. 201. 300. Only one of them has words.

Honeymoon suite

My chest tingles with dread. It doesn't take a genius to figure out what I'm staring at. The DVDs are not random numbers. They're room numbers.

Cole is one sick bastard. He must have recorded people in their hotel rooms.

Grabbing several DVDs, I get to my feet. There are too many for me to carry, but I'll call the cops to get the rest. I'm about to leave the room when I spot another DVD in the box, and the label on it catches my eye.

Guest bedroom

I grab it as well.

I should leave, but now that I've discovered the place that might contain all the evidence, it would be a mistake to get out without covering up my tracks. If Cole shows up before the police get here, I don't want him to know that I found his hiding place so he has time to flee or destroy the evidence I can't carry with me now.

I do my best to spread out the rest of the DVDs in the box to create a flat surface so I can close up their hiding place.

Something tells me I need to act fast and call the police right away.

But what if there's nothing on the DVDs?

Is it possible that I'm wrong? If I call the police, I could end up being the one thrown behind bars. I need to be certain.

Before I slide the floorboards back into their place, I notice something: a photo wedged between two of the boxes. I grip the edge with two fingers and pull it out, then I drop it again with a loud gasp as soon as I take in the memory it captures, the people in it.

It's Brett.

He's lying on what looks like one of the Black Oyster Hotel beds. Next to him is a naked woman and their lips are locked in a kiss.

Not too far away, sitting in a beige armchair with his legs crossed, is Cole, watching.

The woman is Gloria, an eighteen-year-old former maid at the hotel, who quit a month before Brett and I got married. She only worked there for six months, and when she left, there were rumors that she was pregnant.

Not wanting to accept what I'm seeing, I pick up the photo again, hoping that the image will transform into something else.

Slowly, horribly, I feel my heart break and I erupt with an animalistic sound. I run to the wall next to the window and punch it until my knuckles are raw, until I feel dizzy and exhausted. Then I slide down the wall and bury my face between my knees and sob, my eyes burning and nose running.

In the days before Gloria left, she was a shell of her former self, and there was a sadness in her eyes I didn't understand. At the time I thought that maybe there was a loss in her family or something else tragic had happened in her life.

Now it's clear that Brett was the reason for her brokenness.

He was my husband, the man I loved from the moment I saw him, the father of my son. I'm finding it impossible to believe he had a double life, that he was a monster just like his father. He simply couldn't have done all the horrible things that Cole did.

And yet, it's all there in black and white. As much as I'm desperate to bury my head in the sand, the truth is unfolding inside my mind, pieces of the puzzle are clicking into place, the many hours he spent at the hotel, the emergency calls from his father that only he could solve.

I bite my bottom lip, trying to breathe, to manage the emotions raging through me, the headache splitting my head.

I didn't know my husband at all.

The tears refuse to stop, dripping down my chin and into my neck. My head hurts. My entire body hurts. I can't think.

When I'm finally able to catch my breath, I wipe my face with my T-shirt and stand up. Shaking all over with sobs, I put the floorboards back in their place as best I can and reach for my handbag, stuffing the photo into it. Next, I rummage inside for my phone while gazing out the window to make sure the taxi is still outside. It's still there, but I don't see the driver. Dread creeps up on me as I bring my face closer to the glass to better search the darkness.

I don't see it coming.

I don't hear a thing.

I only feel the pain that flares at the back of my skull. My handbag drops to the floor, and I follow it down, my head colliding with the floorboard.

CHAPTER 38

My eyes start to close but not before I see a man coming into view.

Cole.

"I knew you would come." His voice cuts through the silence. He sounds so distant and muffled, but the words are clear. "I left the key for you."

So it was a trap, and I walked straight into it. As I drift in and out of consciousness, it occurs to me that he only mentioned the cabin at the motel because he wanted to remind me of its existence. He let me get away, and he wanted to lure me here. He was a few steps ahead.

The sound of the floorboards creaking as he walks makes my head hurt even more, like there are explosions going off inside it.

Something smashes against the wall. I can't tell whether it's one of the DVDs or some other object. I want to look, but the pain has rendered me immobile.

I'm still trying to push through the pain in my head when more pain ricochets through me—this time in my middle. He's kicked me. Now I'm falling hard and fast into the darkness.

"My son," I whisper, but I'm unable to say more.

"I know where he is," Cole jeers. "When all this is over, I'll bring him here. We'll go hunting together. I'll teach him how to be a man, just like I did with Brett."

"No," I croak. I'm determined to stay, to fight for my son. But when I lift my arm a few inches off the floor, it falls back down. My strength is seeping out of me; I'm trying to grasp hold of it, but I can't.

It's over. I failed Clark. I failed all those women. I failed myself.

Darkness closes over me.

CHAPTER 39

My eyes fly open, and my lungs suck in air. No matter how greedy I am, how much I gulp it in, it's not enough.

Everything is dark except for a blinking red light above me, very close to my face. A camera? When I try to stretch my arms out, they meet a soft surface, some kind of fabric. I force my mind to push through the pain and figure out where I am.

"Welcome back," Cole's voice says. "Be still. Try not to panic or you'll run out of air."

It all comes spinning back to me, and I know that this time, he'll never let me go. He'll kill me, and I'll never see Clark again.

A hot tear slides down the side of my face.

"As soon as I was sure you killed my son, I knew that if I ever found you, you would pay," he continues. "I will do a better job than the police can. Just like I will do a better job raising Ashton than you can."

"What..." I can't speak because my mouth is so dry, and my head is on the verge of exploding.

Why is he still saying I killed Brett when I know he did it?

"Where, you mean? Oh, you're inside your pretty coffin. I had it custom-made for you."

My body stiffens and panic flares up inside me.

He has buried me alive?

"No," I say, but the words only come out in a whisper. "No," I repeat even though it hurts to speak.

"It will be much harder if you resist it. My suggestion is that you should enjoy your last doses of oxygen. Your supply is limited."

"Let me out," I shout. "Please, Cole."

"That's not going to happen."

When I was pregnant with Clark, I read a true-life haunting story about a mall that had collapsed in Michigan, killing dozens of people. It was later reported that some of the victims did not die from being crushed, but from suffocating underneath the rubble. That story haunted me so much that, ever since then, I've been afraid of being buried alive. I remember telling Brett that if I died, I wanted to be cremated to ensure I was really dead. I'd read horror stories of people who woke up in their coffins and ended up dying from lack of oxygen.

Now my life is doomed to end in exactly the way I'd irrationally feared.

My mind goes back to Clark, and I remember Cole telling me that he knows his location. I hope he was only trying to scare me. If he was busy coming after me, how would he know where Tasha took him?

Unless, of course, he paid someone to follow them.

"Don't hurt my son," I say, fresh tears burning my eyes.

"Don't worry, our son will be safe. He'll grow up to be a real man."

I can't let him do it. I can't let him destroy my son.

"He's not yours," I shout, pressing against the silky lining around me. My will to fight rewards me with a huge dose of adrenaline that I use to push against the top of the coffin.

Nothing moves.

"Push harder." He laughs. "Just a little harder."

I know he's playing games with me, he's loving this, but I don't care. I won't go down without a fight.

To my surprise, the cover pops open and air rushes into my lungs. It smells of rotten leaves and wet earth. It's still dark outside, but at least there's more light than inside the closed coffin. I scramble to my feet, my skin crawling. Dizziness makes me fall back, so I crawl out instead and lie on the damp ground, panting as I look up at the moonlight that slices through the leaves of the trees above. At least he didn't bury me yet. I guess he wanted to be able to torment me first.

Move. Save yourself.

Wherever he is, Cole is watching, waiting to pounce.

I roll to my side and then onto my hands and knees, but I almost fall into a deep hole next to the coffin.

I swallow a scream as I kick my feet into the ground and use my hands to move me away from the grave. My grave.

I struggle to my feet, ignoring the pain roiling through my body.

When I start to run blindly into the trees, gulping in the smell of decomposing wood, his laughter rings out behind me. My body is weak, but I keep going, breaking twigs with my bare feet and jumping over logs. I fall a couple of times, but I pick myself up again.

It's only when my lungs start to burn that I stop to listen, to try to determine how far away he is. I no longer hear his voice. The only sound is that of the river.

But not for long.

The sound of pounding feet pursues me.

If he didn't have a limp, he would probably have caught up with me already.

I need to lose him. No matter what, I need to keep moving.

A gunshot slices the night and I fall to the ground as if I have been hit. When I realize I'm fine, I get back on my feet again and continue.

"You won't get away," he shouts behind me. He's close, but I can't turn to look. It will only slow me down.

I keep running until the pain in my chest threatens to stop me, but I have pushed my body to its limit. The trees hide me, but their thorns and branches tear at my skin. My side is screaming at me, begging me to stop running, and I'm forcing my aching legs forward, one after the other. He's still behind me, and I don't know how much longer I can keep going. Where is he getting all his strength from?

"Run, Meghan, run." He laughs. "Run like Brett used to when I chased him. He was a coward even as a kid."

My breath catches in my throat.

This is what he did to his son, what he wants to do to mine?

"Hunting was supposed to teach him how to be a man. He was the prey, and I was the hunter. I always caught up. He never told you, did he?"

I'm reeling from Cole's words, but I need to keep running. I want to stop, to give in to the urge to throw up. But that's not an option. My feet continue to pound the earth, but I feel myself slowing down, and I curse myself for my weakness.

Another bullet splits the silence only moments before a sharp pain strikes my right leg. I bite back a scream when the force of impact stops me in my tracks.

It's over.

Brett once came home from the cabin with a wound in his leg. He told me there was an accident and he refused to go to the hospital.

Now I know the truth. His father shot him, too.

I fall to the ground, writhing with pain. Still determined to get away, I bury my nails into the soil, begging it to move me forward. But nothing happens.

I can make out his footfalls now. He's getting closer.

By the time he reaches me, I'm barely conscious. My eyes

close as soon as he lifts me from the ground, and they only open again when we arrive at the cabin.

I wonder vaguely why he's not taking me to the coffin.

I try to squirm from his grip, but he's strong. He doesn't speak as he drops me into a chair in the living room in front of the TV. Blood is seeping from my wound. I feel it sliding down the back of my leg to the floor, as my body slumps to the side.

He pushes me upright again and ties something around my chest. There's not an ounce of strength left in my body to fight him.

"I hope you enjoyed that little game, Meghan. Now, you came looking for answers," he whispers into my ear. "You're about to get them." When my head lolls forward, he grips my hair and turns my face back to the screen, which is now flickering to life.

My eyes are blurry, but I am forcing myself to watch.

It's a video of him on top of me in the hotel room the night before my wedding. I'm clearly passed out.

He has it on video. Raw anguish spills out of me in a low moan as my wounded heart demands the revenge that it may never find.

After what seems like an eternity, he changes the DVD. The next one is of me and Brett in a bedroom in Nora and Cole's house, making love. I remember that day, two years ago. We had stayed with them for a week while Nora was carrying out some major renovations at our home. I wanted us to stay at the hotel, but Brett insisted we stay with his parents.

Cole had put up cameras in the guest room and watched us the entire time, listening to our conversations.

How sick is this man, and how blind was I not to see it?

The TV goes blank.

Cole tilts his head to the side. "Now that you have the truth you came searching for, it's time for you to die. Your coffin is waiting." He unties the rope from around my body.

I don't know what gets into me, given how shaky and weak I feel, but I jump to my feet, prepared to escape.

"Don't you dare come near me, you monster." My body is vibrating with adrenaline, but my wounded leg refuses to play along. I limp to the back of the chair, daring him to approach me.

"Stop resisting, Meghan. It's over now. No one can save you out here." He pulls a silver handgun from his back pocket and takes a step toward me.

When he comes closer, I muster the little strength I have left to lift the chair, swinging it as hard as I can in his direction and taking him by surprise. It strikes him on the left side of his body.

He growls and drops his gun.

Both our gazes move to the weapon on the floor. It's closer to me than to him. Since I can't walk, I fall over it. He lunges for me as my fingers curl around the gun.

"Goodbye, Meghan." He grabs my hair and drives my head into the floor before snatching the gun from my hand.

I hear a gunshot, and darkness falls around me.

CHAPTER 40

I thought I'd never wake up again, but I do. I can still smell him. His presence is suffocating, but I can't see him.

"Where am I?" I ask even though I'm not sure if anyone is with me.

"You're in the hospital," a woman's voice says. It's familiar, but my memory is foggy and I have to wade through the mess inside my head to place it. When I do, my eyes fill with tears.

"Tasha," I whisper, choking up.

"Are you okay, Zoe?" She comes to my bedside, her eyes sparkling. My vision is blurred, but it's starting to clear.

Without moving my head, which is still hurting, I scan the room. I can tell from the pressure around it that it's bandaged, as is my leg, and my face feels like it's been savaged.

"Where is Clark? Is he safe?" I try to keep the panic from my voice, but it's hard because it's swelling inside me like a balloon trapped in my chest.

"Don't worry." Tasha strokes my cheek. "Clark is fine, he's safe. So are you."

"Where is he? Where's Cole? Did I manage to shoot him? Did he shoot me again?"

"He was shot by the police." She wipes her cheek. "They got to him just in time."

I blink at her, confused.

"He's dead?" I bite into my trembling bottom lip.

"No, Mrs. Wilton," a man answers from the doorway. "But you never have to worry about him again." He stretches out a hand to shake mine. "I'm Detective Jason Rogers."

The red-headed forty-something detective is tall with pale skin and a hint of stubble on his jaw. His eyes are so dark they look black.

"You saved my life?" My hand feels weak in his grip.

"No, a taxi driver called the police." He loosens his navy tie. "He said he drove you to the cabin, and someone stabbed him. Unfortunately, he was in a very bad way and he didn't make it. But if it weren't for him, you might not have either."

An innocent person is dead because of me. That's all I can think about, and I break down. My tears soak into the pillow, but I don't care. I almost wish I could pass out again, so I wouldn't have to live with the intense guilt and shame I feel, the horror pulsing through my mind that keeps rushing back to the coffin, the trees, my helplessness as Cole tortured me. But I hang on for Clark.

The detective gives me the time I need to cry for the man who saved my life, and Tasha strokes my back in silence until I feel somewhat better.

"Cole did it," I say finally. "I found evidence to prove he raped a lot of women, including me. There were DVDs and a photo."

"We know that now. And we also know that your husband was involved. So were many other powerful men who visited the hotel."

I wipe my eyes. It's all too much to take in. "I didn't kill my husband," I say finally.

The detective nods his head. "We are now pursuing a different lead."

"I'm really innocent," I continue, not really processing his words and holding tightly on to Tasha's hand. "I think Cole did it. Maybe he was afraid that Brett would come clean."

The man nods with a smile. "We do now believe you are innocent, yes. But even though Cole Wilton did some terrible things, he didn't kill his son. He was at his hotel with—" he clears his throat. "One of the DVDs you found was recorded that night."

*

The next day, Clark steps into my hospital room. He's holding a teddy bear I haven't seen before, and he looks somehow smaller than when I last saw him. "Mommy, Mommy." He rushes to my bedside. With tears in his eyes, he places his little hand on my forehead. "Don't die."

"No." I smile at him through my tears. "That won't happen. I'm not going anywhere."

Tasha has sworn to keep my secret, and I haven't told the detective I came close to killing Brett that night, and even prepared the syringe. I know how it will look. But now that they know what Brett did, and after finding evidence to show he bought the cyanide, they believe he did it himself. I suspect that Cole and Nora put pressure on the police to pursue me before, but now their power has been broken.

I'm not going to mention how weak Brett was that night, far too weak to lift up his arm.

I spoke to a lawyer over the phone, who promised to do everything to clear my name of any charges. She doubted anything would happen to me.

"What's that?" I ask, noticing an object Clark is holding in his other hand.

"It's an injection. The nurse gave it to me. But it's not a real one."

"Do you want to make Mommy better?" I ask, remembering the game he used to play with Brett.

He shakes his head. "No, I don't want to." His voice is trembling now.

"Why not? You can pretend you're the doctor. I'm your patient."

"But I don't want you to leave and go to heaven."

I frown. "Baby, what do you mean? I won't go anywhere."

"But Daddy did."

"Yes, because he was very sick. He was in a lot of pain."

Clark nods and drops his head. "I wanted to make his pain go away, but he went to get better in heaven."

"You tried to make Daddy's pain go away?" A cold shower of realization hits me. "What do you mean, baby?"

After a long silence, he speaks. "Daddy said if I inject him, he will not have pain anymore."

I sit up and the room starts to spin. "You... you tried to make Daddy better? You injected him?"

"Yes. He was crying, and I went to cuddle him. I saw an injection on the floor. Daddy said there was special medicine inside to help him feel better. He wanted me to give it to him."

"You... you..." my voice trails off and my mouth suddenly feels like dry, dusty paper. "Did he tell you how to do it?"

Clark nods. "We did it together just like when we used to play doctor games. Daddy was holding my hand and we pushed the needle into his arm. I helped him get the medicine." He crawls up to lie next to me in the hospital bed, and when I wrap my arms around him, I'm trembling.

Brett asked our son to kill him?

Shock and hurt surge through me and heat rises in my face. It is utterly incomprehensible to me that Brett would ask a child to do such a monumental thing, something that he didn't even understand, and that could cause him so much trauma and pain later in life.

I feel like I've been punched in the stomach.

But the horrible truth is, part of me feels that I'm equally responsible for what happened. Clark would not have injected his father if I was still in that room. If I had stayed with Brett to the end.

EPILOGUE

ONE YEAR LATER

I sit on the grass, enjoying the touch of the breeze as it sweeps through my hair. The blades of green underneath my feet feel like heaven, and above me the bright-blue sky is the perfect backdrop to a peaceful day. I soak it in, the energy around me, the earth holding me up, the world full of life and beauty.

"Please could I have some more juice?" Clark asks and I smile, reaching for his plastic cup.

The picnic was his idea. He hates being indoors, and I understand. Now that he's free to be a kid again, we are outside a lot making up for lost time. At a distance, several children are playing. A few minutes ago, Clark played with some of them and watching him warmed my heart and broke it at the same time. He's still a child like the others, but at the same time, I know he has been robbed of his innocence.

Sometimes I catch him staring into the distance, deep in thought, and I pray that what he's thinking about has nothing to do with what happened. I'd give anything to see inside his head, to erase the dark memories, so he can live his life without a constant reminder of the nightmare he went through hanging over his head.

I'll never tell anyone how Brett really died. But my greatest fear is that even though I'm trying to protect my son, he will never forget that night. And even if he does, it will come back to him one day.

Brett was for sure his father, although, of course, I'm no longer proud of that. A DNA test proved that Clark was not Cole's. Anyway, I am determined that he will never turn out like either of them.

In the courtroom and the newspapers, I discovered a lot of things about Cole's childhood that he'd never told anyone about. He was born and raised in Beaufort, South Carolina, by a father who was an oyster farmer, and a mother who physically and emotionally abused them both. His mother was responsible for the injury that resulted in his limp, when she broke his leg with a spade. He had just finished high school when his father killed his wife, and then himself.

Cole left Beaufort after their deaths and went to the University of Florida. He graduated with honors and later worked for a major luxury hotel chain until he decided to open up his Black Oyster chain of hotels. The prosecutor said he had been raping and abusing women for years, fueled by his own mother's cruelty.

I push Cole to the back of my mind. However dark one's past is, it does not give anyone the license to harm others.

All I care about is that the slate has been wiped clean and I can try to move on. The court has declared me not guilty, and Clark and I can live our lives without fear. Cole no longer has the power to hurt us.

For Clark's sake, I'm learning to embrace life, even with the scars I'll always have on my heart.

When Clark finishes his drink, he hugs me and runs off to play some more. His laughter floats back to me when he chases after a girl with pigtails. He looks so happy, but for how long?

I shake my head. I can't think about it now. When the time

comes, I'll be there to hold him. I will do everything in my power to make sure he knows what happened was not his fault.

I throw back my head and gaze up at the sky, watching the soft clouds moving and forming shapes. My eyes follow a lone bird that flies high above, its wings stretched out, soaring through the clouds. It reminds me of the freedom Cole lost, now that he's trapped behind bars. He's in a high-security prison, serving a life sentence with no chance of parole. He confessed to killing Denise, who had repeatedly threatened to go to the cops.

During his trial, it was revealed that Nora knew all along what her husband and son were doing, that she hid evidence and paid maids to keep their mouths shut. She was the person who set fire to the hotel in order to destroy any kind of evidence from being discovered; it wasn't the protesters as everyone initially believed.

A week after she was also locked up, Clark and I returned to Willow Creek to try to live a quiet life. It's our new home now. I decided to keep the name Zoe, preferring to leave Meghan in the past, in her happy ignorance of all the horrors around and within her.

When Clark finishes playing, we get into our car and drive home. Ruth left me everything she had owned. The house, some savings, and even the cabin all belong to me now. Maybe deep down, she knew I was innocent and wanted to help me rebuild my life.

Clark was thrilled to be able to live permanently in the fairy-tale house, and in memory of Ruth, I haven't changed a thing. Not the furniture, not the flowery wallpaper, not even the curtains. For as long as possible, I want both of us to feel like Ruth is still with us, to better be able to imagine her walking around the home she used to love, opening the pink fridge or sitting at the kitchen table, leafing through the paper with a cup of coffee in front of her.

I used some of the money to open Ruth's Bakery, located on the same street as Lemon, where I also deliver freshly baked goods every morning. I wanted the bakery to feel like a home to anyone who walks in, so I decorated it in bright and bold colors, with happy and vibrant patterns, and the glass-fronted cases display the different types of bread and pastries I bake. On one of the walls is a large, framed black and white photo of Ruth, the woman who encouraged me to follow my dream. I know she would have been so proud and happy for me.

Coming back home from the park, it still feels strange now to walk down the path from the gate to the front door of Ruth's old home. Sometimes I expect her to walk out.

When Clark is playing video games in his room after lunch, I go to my bedroom and switch on my computer. After being approached many times by publishers, I'm finally ready to share my story. The book I'm writing is almost done, but I left the title for last. With only one chapter left to go, I finally type it in.

The Missing Widow.

It's perfect.

I position my hands on the keyboard again and start to write the epilogue. Before I can finish, I glance at a box in the corner and my eyes land on a manila envelope that for the past year I've dreaded opening.

Maybe I'm ready for that too.

The envelope was in a secret safe in the house, just as Brett told me it would be. I'm surprised the cops didn't find it when they were looking for evidence against me, but I guess Brett always was good at hiding things. I had expected to find money and fake passports inside, but when I finally got my hands on it, I knew it was too thin.

I spill the contents onto the bed, but only one sheet of paper slides out.

Meghan,

I'm sure you thought you would find something different, something to help you run from the law if the cops find out you killed me. I'm sorry to disappoint you. I won't be giving you the escape you need.

I asked you to kill me for a reason.

The truth is out, Meghan. I know what you did with my father the night before our wedding. A little while ago, he told me everything. He showed me photos.

You probably know by now that I have done some terrible things, things I'm not proud of. What you don't know is that you changed me. When I met you, I became a different man, a better man. Everything I did was before I married you. Because of you, I gave up my old ways.

I thought you were different, but I was wrong. Like so many other women, you were defenseless to my father's charms. He told me how you flirted with him, offered him champagne, and invited him to the honeymoon suite.

He said Ashton is not my son, but his. Did you think I'd never find out?

I can't believe you would do that to me.

I'm dying, but I want you to suffer once I'm gone. I want you to go to prison.

The one thing my father did right in his life is showing me the true colors of the woman I married.

I drop the letter to the floor, my mind spinning.

I know the day Cole told Brett his twisted version of the truth. It was the day he was called out for an emergency and came back a changed man, when he started pulling away from me and Clark. The night he asked me to help him die.

"Mommy, Mommy," Clark calls. "There's a squirrel in our garden. Come and look."

"I'm coming." I bite down on my lip until it stings.

In a daze, I get to my feet, barely able to hold myself up. I make it to the garden in one piece and pretend to be excited about the squirrel, but my heart feels like it's gone, ripped from my chest, and my tears are close to the surface. For Clark's sake, I try to hold myself together.

As the hours pass, I sneak away from time to time to cry in private and reread the letter. But the words don't change, and with each word I read, I feel more broken and betrayed as the tears race down my cheeks.

When night falls, I put Clark to bed and head downstairs to wash the dishes, relieved that I can finally be alone to process my emotions.

The first thing I notice as I reach the last step on the stairs is the smell of coffee, even though I didn't make any today. The second thing is the sound of crockery clinking.

My heart is racing as I walk barefoot on the cool tiles to the kitchen. With trembling hands, I push open the door.

Someone is hunched over the kitchen table, dressed in black, her back turned to me. A thick, dark braid falls from the back of a black and white baseball cap and down her back like a snake.

I blink in shock, then take a step toward her.

"Jane?" I croak, my voice weak. I haven't seen her since the night Brett died.

Jane lifts a cup of coffee to her lips and takes a drink before turning to face me. Her eyes are red-rimmed and swollen as if she's been crying.

"Hello, Mrs. Wilton." She glances at her lap, and when I do the same, my eyes land on a knife, and the blade sparkles as it catches the light.

My eyes widen, and I back up as she stands and takes a step forward, the knife now raised in her hand.

"What are you doing?" I ask, my eyes darting around,

searching for something to defend myself with. "How did you—"

"I came to remind you that you're just as guilty as your husband and his father." Her finger traces the blade of the knife.

"I didn't... I didn't know anything. Jane, you have to believe me." I back away, my eyes fixed on the knife. It looks sharp enough to slice through flesh like butter.

"Like you believed us when we told you not to marry that sick rapist?" Her voice cracks, and tears streak down her cheeks as she drops back into the chair she had been sitting on. "You willingly became one of them."

As I shake my head, I bite back tears. "I didn't know. I am so sorry for what they did to you and—"

"Denise?" She wipes at her tears and lifts her shoulders before letting them drop again. "Sorry can't bring her back. It's too little too late, Meghan. Wounds can heal, but scars never go away. They are always there, reminding you of the pain."

I shake my head and sniff. "Why? Why are you doing this?" I ask, my voice quivering.

I'm barely able to breathe as she gets to her feet again and steps toward me, her eyes on the knife in her hand.

"I've been watching you get away with it all, while you, too, are responsible for Denise's death. I blame you completely for doing nothing, for letting them get away with it. You have her blood on your hands."

"No!" Tears flood my eyes. "I swear I had nothing to do with it. She was also my friend. *You* were my friend. I helped you both get jobs—"

She smacks her forehead. "Oh, yes, that's right. You helped me get hired so your future husband and father-in-law could violate me and lend me to their disgusting guests." She inhales sharply. "You knew what was going on in that place, just like

Nora did. Those special guests paid extra, didn't they? Did some of it go into your pocket?"

"I... Jane..." My voice drifts off as I bury my hands in my hair and let out a sob. "I'm so sorry, but I swear I didn't know. I wasn't even dating Brett at the time. Come on; we lived together. It would have been hard to hide something like that from you."

"You liar!" she screams, her voice echoing in the silent kitchen. "I know you two were dating secretly." She wipes the sweat from her upper lip. "I'm happy your bastard husband is dead. I only agreed to work for you because I wanted to kill him myself. I spent ages figuring out how to do it and get away with it. But then the stomach cancer got there first, and I couldn't believe my luck." A grin creeps onto her lips. "He got what he deserved, and I'm so proud of myself for scaring him out of getting chemo."

"It was you?" I gasp. "You convinced him not to do chemo?"

"I didn't want him to have a way out. And it was so much fun watching him waste away day by day until, of course, you killed him."

"I didn't," I whisper. "Brett committed suicide. The police confirmed it a year ago."

"I know, but you filled that syringe and put it within his reach." She shakes her head and grips the knife tighter. "That's the only right thing you ever did. And now, his parents are also paying for their crimes. So there's only one Wilton left who didn't get what they deserve. You." As she says the word, she stabs the air between us, the tip of the knife pointing at me.

I hold up my hands in defense, my palms facing her, and plead with my eyes as my feet stumble back until I hit the wall. "Please, don't do this... you don't want to kill me. Let's just talk."

"I should have done it long ago when a friend told me where you were. In my hometown of all places." Her eyes are narrow, her lips set in a thin line. "When I found you, I wanted to hurt you, but then it was so much fun to watch you scared of your shadow." She smiles bitterly. "The months after Cole and Nora went to prison, I thought maybe that justice was served, that it was enough, and I should just let you be. But I couldn't... I can't let you go unpunished."

"So you want to kill me?" My voice is barely a whisper as tears stream down my cheeks. "Please, Jane. I have a son—"

"Denise had a child too." She spits the words out like venom. "She was pregnant when she was murdered."

I wince in horror. "Please," I beg again, "you don't want to do this. Let's talk about it."

"There's nothing to talk about. It's too late, Meghan. You need to pay for what you did."

"You're not a killer, Jane." Sweat drips down my back, and my breathing is ragged.

"You're right, I'm not." A faint smile plays on her lips. "But *you* are." In one fluid movement, she takes my hand and wraps my fingers around the knife. I'm too shocked to resist, and it all happens so quickly. With her hand around mine, she takes the knife to her neck and cuts it across.

I scream and close my eyes as I hear a loud thump echo through the room. I force myself to open my eyes and I see Jane on the floor, blood spilling out of the gash on her neck, a horrible gargling sound coming from her throat.

Her eyes flicker for a few seconds and then go still, but they remain wide open. They continue to stare up at my hand, the one holding the knife.

A LETTER FROM L.G. DAVIS

Dear reader,

I want to thank you for taking the time to read *The Missing Widow*. The process of creating Meghan's character, putting obstacles in her way, and watching her overcome them was very rewarding for me, even if it was also challenging at times.

The fictional town of Willow Creek was also a lot of fun to bring to life. I hope it's a town that, if it were real, you would have loved to visit on your next vacation, to stop for a drink or a meal at the Lemon Café & Restaurant or a sweet treat at Ruth's Bakery.

In my next book, I hope to introduce you to more memorable characters and locations, shocking reveals and gripping twists. To be notified when my next novel comes out, please sign up at the link below. Your email address will never be shared, and you can unsubscribe anytime.

www.bookouture.com/l-g-davis

If you enjoyed reading *The Missing Widow* as much as I enjoyed writing it, I'd love it if you would consider posting a review. It would be wonderful to hear your thoughts, and you would also be helping other readers decide whether this book is for them. Thank you in advance for your time.

It's always a pleasure to connect with my readers. You can find me on my Facebook page, follow me on Instagram or Twitter, or visit my website. Please do contact me with any questions, feedback, or just to say hello. I look forward to hearing from you.

Thank you again for reading.

Much love,

Liz xxx

http://www.author-lgdavis.com

 facebook.com/LGDavisBooks
twitter.com/LGDavisAuthor
instagram.com/LGDavisAuthor

ACKNOWLEDGMENTS

I could not have written this book without the support of my family, friends, and the fantastic Bookouture team.

I want to thank my family, especially my husband and children, for their patience through the long hours of writing and editing this book, and for encouraging me whenever I doubted myself. You are my inspiration, and I love you so much.

Thank you to my brilliant editor, Rhianna Louise, for pushing me to produce a book I felt proud of. You are an amazing person, and I appreciate you for being a true champion of my work. Having you by my side is priceless. I couldn't have done it without you.

Additionally, I would like to thank the entire Bookouture team, who worked tirelessly on polishing the manuscript, designing the cover, marketing, and launching the book. You are all incredibly talented, and I am honored to be in your company. Thank you in particular to Donna Hillyer, Jess Readett, Alexandra Holmes, Emily Boyce, Alex Crow, Alba Proko, and everyone else who was involved in this process.

Finally, I want to thank my readers for allowing me to continue doing what I love. It is because of you that I have come this far, and I always feel humbled to be able to share my stories with you. You keep me writing that next word, sentence, and chapter.

Thank you, truly, from the bottom of my heart.

Printed in Great Britain
by Amazon

36765657R00142